Stiletto Hell

Stiletto Hell

DiVitto Kelly

Stiletto Hell

Copyright © 2020 DiVitto Kelly

Content Editor: Amanda Clarke
Copy Editor: Cortney Rowe
Cover Art: Fiona Kelly-Lopez
Editor-in-Chief: Kristi King-Morgan
Formatting: Kristi King-Morgan
Assistant Editor: Maddy Drake

ISBN- 978-1-947381-32-2

www.dreamingbigpublications.com

Table of Contents

Stiletto Hell

Harold Bailey dashed into the second-floor bathroom and slammed the door shut, fumbling with the old-fashioned key before securing it. The forty-two-year-old man trembled as he reached for his cell phone with his sweaty hands, dialing the appropriate three-digit number before accidently dropping it on the tile floor; luckily it didn't break.

"Come, come on," he screamed as he picked it up. "Answer the phone! Hello?"

"Denville Police department, what is your emergency?" said the female voice, cool and firm.

"I'm being attacked!" bellowed Harold. He was normally mild-mannered and predictable, but this was too much.

Whack, whack, whack; each time louder. Small fragments of the door were splintering in every direction. Harold's eyes grew as big as cue balls in horror.

"They're coming for me, you gotta help!" he shrieked, cowering in fear, now crouching in the antique white bathtub.

"An intruder is breaking in, sir?" the voice asked.

"Kinda sorta," stammered Harold, trying to maintain his composure. "It's a pair of killer red stiletto shoes with heels six inches long. They're trying to murder me!"

Another whack!

""I'm sorry, did you say stiletto heels, sir? Is someone trying to harm you with a pair of shoes? Is this a prank?"

asked the woman. It was October 30, also known as mischief night, a pre-Halloween ritual where kids toilet papered neighbor's trees, egged houses, and occasionally blew up in mailboxes with M-80s.

"No, I swear," replied Harold, sweating bullets despite the chill in the three-story, hundred-year-old house. He stood up but slipped on a half-used bar of Irish Spring, skating right out of the tub and landing flat on his back. The phone went flying, a three pointer straight into the toilet. Splash.

"Son of a bitch!" groaned Harold. He struggled to sit up then reached into the bowl to retrieve his phone, drying it off quickly with a hand towel.

"I'm sorry, what did you just call me?" bellowed the voice.

"I didn't mean you. Look, I . . ."

The emergency call operator was already boiling over in annoyance. It wasn't the first prank phone call she'd received tonight. Her last call had been that the town was being invaded by alien squirrels. She hung up on Harold and went back to her game of computer solitaire.

"Noooo!" howled Harold. Trying to regain his composure, he placed the phone in his back pocket. He slowly turned towards the door. There was silence. *Have they stopped?* Four piercing holes in the door created a textbook 'connect the dot' square. Harold picked up the toilet bowl scrub brush and inched forward. He approached the door, bracing his left foot at the bottom.

"Where are you, you abomination of women's footwear?" he snarled, leaning closer. He squinted his right eye through one of the holes for a better view. There on the floor, pointed directly at him, was a lone, gleaming red stiletto.

Hold on, I only see one of you, but where's the other?

SLAM. The other stiletto heel torpedoed straight through the door, spearing Harold's left thigh and penetrating the flesh before darting away. Harold wailed in pain as he backed away, now bleeding profusely from the wound.

"You bastard!" He dropped to the floor, clutching his thigh as blood seeped through his fingertips. He grabbed a hand towel from the brass hoop holder and pressed hard to stop the flow.

He dragged himself over to the cabinet below the sink and scurried for bandages. *Where the hell are they?* He scooped everything out with his arm and littered the bathroom floor with the contents. *Flashlight, bath toys, soap, cotton balls, dryer, and Band-Aids. Yes!*

Harold stood up then pulled down his pants to examine the injury. *Oh, for Christ's sake!* "I'm gonna turn you little shits into Hush Puppies!"

He doused the wound with hydrogen peroxide and dried it off before applying two of the larger Band-Aids side by side to cover the gash. Harold applied a few strips of white bandage tape for good measure. He pulled up his jeans and staggered over to the sink, his thigh throbbing in pain.

He opened the mirrored cabinet door and snatched the bottle of Tylenol. *Let's see, the proper dosage for . . . what the hell am I doing?* He quickly popped four into his mouth and chased it down with water from a kiddie cup. He placed his hands on each side of the sink and slowly raised his head. He stared straight into the mirror, a light smear of blood painted his jawline. *Alright shoes; your sole is mine.* He let out a crazed laugh with just the right touch of wicked.

***

The size seven pair of soaring, primeval pumps were a gift from one of his wife's schoolteacher friends.

Harold's wife, Kathy, was the librarian at the K-8 Saint Anthony Catholic School and was still firmly smitten with the preppy look of the 1980's. She never wore high heels, maybe an inch at the most, and that was daring. For a playful joke, Christina Watkins, the always effervescent and uniquely dressed art teacher, decided to spice things up in Kathy's humdrum 'podiatry' lifestyle.

On a sunny Saturday fall afternoon trip to the Village in New York City, Christina had spotted a wicked pair of deep red stiletto shoes at Madam Celeste's Sidewalk Shoe Emporium. The devilishly looking proprietor with long black hair and garbed in a paisley tapestry dress flashed a crooked, toothy grin. Christina couldn't resist, plopping down a pair of wrinkled twenty-dollar bills.

A week later at her surprise birthday party, Kathy had opened the silver-wrapped gift box, completely bowled over. "Now this is me," she laughed.

After relentless prodding and multiple rounds of Sea Breezes and Screwdrivers, Kathy finally caved, giddy and drunk enough to give them a test walk.

She slipped off her favorite pair of bubble gum pink Van's sneakers and stepped into the uncertainty of skyscraper footwear. After some trial and error, her legs wobbling a bit, Kathy stood proudly like a stilt walker, now towering over her husband by four inches, maybe more.

Harold could only muster up a half-hearted smile. He was self-conscious about his below average height, a notch under five foot six. He preferred his wife's taste in no-heel shoes, which made him appear taller.

The whole thing got Harold wondering, and not in a good way. What if his mild-mannered wife of thirteen years embraced the stilettos and suddenly transformed herself into a mischievous, sinful babe, strutting around in those sultry, hot-rod shoes? And what if clean-cut Kathy decided teaching to a bunch of snot-nosed elementary school children was a wee bit too mundane for her newfound party girl lifestyle. He could already see her chiming, snapping on bubble gum, wrists clanging with cheap fourteen-carat gold jewelry. "Harold honey, from now on, I'm gonna flaunt my flesh for some serious Do-Re-Mi. Ca-Ching!"

No, no, and hell no! Mister Harold Bailey, a very average human being, was going to make sure those shoes never touched her feet again.

***

Harold staggered to the door once again, this time with a bit more awareness. He leaned in again and took in a deep breath. There on the floor stood the right shoe, tapping incessantly on the light parquet wood floor. He scratched the door with the scrub brush, hoping to provoke the devil shoe to attack. And right on target, the metallic red spear bayonetted the wood door, breaking through.

But this time, Harold was ready. He seized the shoe, smothering the hostile heel with a towel, before wrestling it to the bathroom floor. The shoe stopped moving.

Suddenly, it bolted off the floor, nearly pulling Harold's arms out of their sockets as it desperately flew in every direction like a captured hawk. Harold hung on for dear life. He stuck to his guns, finally dragging the shoe down into the toilet. He stuffed the bundled-up towel inside, slammed the lid down and ran rings of bandage tape around the bowl. For good measure, he flushed the toilet a half-dozen times. The shoe banged violently against the porcelain enclosure then simmered down. *Did it drown? Was it dead?* Harold pondered for a moment. *Hold on, how the hell can a shoe can be alive in the first place!*

With the right shoe secured, it was on to the left. He peered out one of the holes in the door but didn't see a thing. He dragged the scrub brush against the door, hoping to entice it. Nothing. It was gone.

The lights cut out. Harold fumbled for the flashlight on the floor. He flicked it on; thankfully it worked.

The house was dead quiet; his wife and kids wouldn't be home for at least another two hours. Harold opened the door as gently as possible. The old hinges squeaked no matter how much he showered them with WD-40. He hobbled over to the bannister near the top of the steps, his jeans soaked in blood.

His ears perked up as he caught a faint noise coming from the kitchen. Harold turned off the flashlight and limped down each step like a senior citizen, prodding along at a snail's pace. At the halfway point, he paused, his eyes becoming more accustomed to the darkness. The fireplace flickered with short bursts of dark orange flames, starving for more wood.

Harold gingerly ambled down the hallway leading to the kitchen. Nothing there. He sighed. Harold took a few more steps before his injured leg nearly gave out. The pain was excruciating. He finally regrouped when he heard a peculiar sound emanating from downstairs. Holding the small flashlight in his right hand, Harold clutched the railing as he managed the narrow staircase leading into the dark basement. Unnoticed, he hobbled quietly over to check on the fuse box. It was smashed to bits, like someone had taken a hammer and pounded away repeatedly.

"Crapola," Harold uttered. He turned, looking around. There had to be something he could use to defeat the possessed shoes.

Harold went into the garage and scrounged around for his fishing equipment. There, stuffed in a five-gallon orange bucket, was a circular, five-foot in diameter nylon cast net with inch-long weights lined along the ends. He grabbed the net, a handsaw, and his son's beat-up hockey stick, then trudged back upstairs.

Harold stumbled over to the fireplace and dropped a couple of split logs and newspaper onto the dying fire. It perked up almost immediately, providing much better visibility. He shifted his deep brown recliner to the side, backed into a corner, and opened the net like an inviting spider web.

"Time to meet your cobbler," growled Harold. The only sounds emanating from the old house were of Harold's drumbeating heart and the crackling of dried wood now bursting into flames.

At the top of the stairs, a pronounced tap echoed throughout the old house. Harold's heartbeat kicked into overdrive. Tap. Tap. Tap. The sound was methodically paced, almost like a metronome, approaching each step with paused perfection. Through the railings, Harold could make out the light of the flames reflecting off the metallic red material.

Both shoes appeared at the bottom of the stairs. They stood side by side, pointing directly at Harold. For a moment he thought of the glistening ruby red (and completely harmless) slippers from *The Wizard of Oz*. He was fairly certain Dorothy would have shunned stilettos.

The shoes inched closer, taking short, measured steps. Harold prepped the cast net, grasping one part in his hands, the other with his teeth. There were still frayed morsels of dried seaweed attached to the crisscrossing lines. It even had the effervescent flavor of Jersey shore. The foes stared at each other down, as much as shoes could stare. It was the O.K. Corral, *Twilight Zone* style.

Without warning, the stilettos jettisoned from the floor like cannon balls, the pointed heels zooming straight for Harold's balding head. He dropped the net in fright, diving out of the way just in time. But he managed to tangle the deadly heels up like trapped baitfish

Getting to his feet, Harold raised the hockey stick and started pummeling the shoes into submission. One managed to scurry away, but the other remained, hampered by its broken heel. He dropped to his knees and brandished the handsaw like a maniac. He peeled back the net, grabbed the shoe mid-high at the heel and started sawing away.

Deep crimson blood spilled over his clutching fingers. "What the hell?" Harold gasped. The wounded footwear pulsated in his hand . . . it felt like a beating heart. He dropped it in disgust. It started moving – throbbing. He stared at the freakish object before picking it up with the fireplace tongs and dropped it into the fire. The shoe let out an ear-piercing squeal before erupting into flames.

Before Harold could even catch his breath, he recognized a familiar grinding sound emitting from the kitchen. He stood up, clutching the hockey stick in his right hand. Galvanized by killing one of the shoes, Harold marched over to the remodeled kitchen, full of stainless-steel appliances and hanging pots and pans.

"No way," he said, almost mouthing the words in disbelief. The stiletto was sharpening its lethal heel, the tip almost glowing hot. Harold plucked the large hanging black metal skillet and held it firmly. The malicious stiletto abruptly stopped and turned towards him.

Harold gritted his teeth. *One down, one to go.* He raised the iron skillet and bellowed. "Well, whatcha gonna do – shoe?"

The stiletto took off like a slap shot, but Harold blocked it cleanly with the heavy-duty cooking utensil. The shoe dropped harmlessly to the floor. He dropped down on all fours and roared, pounding the shoe into submission so much so he cracked two of the new Spanish tiles.

Scrambling along the kitchen counter, Harold snagged an oven mitt and picked up the stiletto. He held it up for closer inspection. "How the hell are you doing this?"

He felt a familiar pulsing sensation. The shoe twisted slowly in his cumbersome grip, baring the pointed heel directly at his face. In a panic, Harold dropped the shoe to the ground. He reached for the iron skillet again, ready to pummel the shoe when it vanished from view.

"Damn-it!" shouted Harold. "Where the hell did you go?"

He found out seconds later as the killer stiletto brought its pointed heel straight down on his foot, easily piercing through his LL Bean low-cut duck boots. Harold wailed in pain. He had had enough.

Running off a string of expletives, he grabbed the shoe, pulling it out from his own bleeding flesh like a stubborn backyard weed. Harold shifted over to the microwave on the counter and tossed the shoe inside. He went to cook the hell out of the stiletto, forgetting about the power outage. Outraged, he picked up the small appliance and rattled it over his head like a crazed lunatic.

Harold hobbled over to the living room, still clutching the microwave, and stood in front of the fireplace. Hearing silence from the microwave, he popped open the door and reached in. He snatched out the shoe then proceeded to drop it into the fireplace. He stood still as the roasting footwear squirmed and screeched in the flames. A reddish cloud suddenly emerged from the barbequed shoe before dissipating up through the chimney. He reached in with the tongs.

"Looks like the other shoe has dropped," proclaimed Harold as he inspected what was left of the evil footwear.

Harold struggled over to the hallway bathroom where he washed and rinsed his wounds. He went into the kitchen and opened the refrigerator, reaching for two bottles of Molson Golden before retreating to the recliner where he plopped down his weary body. Harold strategically placed one of the cold beers on his throbbing thigh wound, the other consumed in victory.

He dropped a couple more logs in the fireplace, sat back down and watched them burn.

"Guess you won't be setting foot in my house ever again."

Employees of BuyMart

It wasn't exactly a festive Sunday evening for Ben and Ellie Gardner. He needed to pick up medicine for Ellie, who was suffering from a nasty cough, congestion, and a runny nose that wouldn't stop running. Ben wasn't feeling so hot either. Apparently, all the fresh mountain air of Falls Creek, North Carolina wasn't agreeing with them.

So far, the early summer weather felt cool and refreshing. The couple, originally from sticky, humid Miami, had recently pulled up stakes and relocated to the quaint town, a two-hour drive north of Charlotte. The Gardners were three months new to the area, enjoying the refreshing change of climate, but one thing that immediately took getting use to was driving far and wide to the nearest anything. Before, trips to the doctor's office, grocery store, or gas station were always within a mile or two. Now, they practically needed a GPS to go anywhere.

The alternative would be moving back to the Sunshine State, but they'd had their fill with the stifling heat and hurricanes, not to mention the robberies, three to be precise. No, a little driving was fine. Having the convertible top down on their gecko green VW Beetle in the Carolina cool was well worth the extra travel time.

Their former home in Miami was a two-bedroom, one-bath bungalow with a hint of Art Deco flair. The corner property was a mini tropical paradise with native Florida plants and citrus trees soaking up the sun in about every crevice of their fenced-in yard. But the third and final robbery was the last straw.

The young couple craved a bit more normalcy. And they found it. The new neighborhood was one part trendy, one part Mayberry, a quaint parcel of town distinguished by its friendliness, historic downtown, and a barbeque joint named the Southern Pig that served up *the* best pulled pork sandwich Ben had ever tasted.

Their new home was twenty years new and spacious: two stories, three bedrooms, two baths, a fireplace, and a lofty oak tree in the front yard big enough for a tire swing, a specific request made by their daughter. Ellie had relatives in nearby Carrboro, which made relocating to the Tar Heel State a less harrowing task to manage.

"Are you sure you don't mind?" said Ellie, her cough approaching sea lion-esque proportions. She looked at the clock – 12:17AM exactly. "Ugh." And she had to be at work in less than seven hours – double ugh.

Ben slipped on his worn blue jeans and Miami Heat long sleeved t-shirt. "Don't be silly. Besides, it'll give me a chance to pick up a box of those chocolate-peanut butter Pop-Tarts; they look tantalizing."

"Don't you dare," replied his wife, lying miserably in their queen-sized bed. "You keep whining about your love handles – it's time to start eating like an adult."

Ben had introduced their six-year-old daughter Sophia to the rectangular pastries, and she loved them too, especially the cinnamon frosted ones. Like father, like daughter.

"Bah humbug," he said. "Besides, I've been doing my sit-ups regularly, see?" Ben pulled up his shirt, showing off his partially svelte frame. "Not too bad."

Ellie fluffed her pillow and sat up. "Do you know what medicine to get?"

"Sudafed, right?" answered Ben.

Ellie's bleary eyes were itchy and irritated, her nose tomato red from all the excessive blowing. "Nah, get Nyquil Cold and Flu, and make sure it's the nighttime stuff; I need to sleep"

Ben finished tying his sneakers. "Anything else?"

"Chamomile tea would be nice, the one with the bear zonked out on the recliner."

"Got it. How do I get to BuyMart again?" Ben had an incredible knack for getting lost. *Thank God for GPS*, he thought.

"Go left out of the driveway, drive about ten miles, then make a left at the blinking light. Make another left at Fletcher Street, then a right on River Road; you can't miss it," replied Ellie, who'd been there at least two dozen times already. She applied more Vapor Rub to her upper chest and added a touch just under her tender nose. Ben jotted everything down on the back of a grocery store receipt.

"You know, I've never been there late at night," said Ben, who'd been told by fellow coworkers at his job at the community college that things got creepy after the sun went down, especially after the witching hour. He had been introduced to the People of BuyMart website by his jocular co-workers and had to admit it was 'interesting.' There appeared to be something a bit off kilter about this particular store. He couldn't explain it.

"Wish me luck, honey."

"You have your cell?"

"Uh, I do now," Ben replied, picking it up off his dresser. "Seal you soon."

"Very funny," barked Ellie. "Oh, would you mind picking up some canned sardines for me too? The ones packed in olive oil. I could use a salty treat."

Ben grimaced. He despised the smell of those tiny tin-housed fishies. "Then I get to buy my Pop-Tarts."

"Your choice, Senior Lipid."

"Everyone loves a good fat cell joke." Ben replied with a grin. He donned his Miami Marlins baseball cap backwards to conceal his springy, black curly hair. "I'm off!"

Ben drove down the gravel strewn driveway and made a left onto the meandering ten-mile stretch of road, forests encroaching on both sides. He loved the dips and turns of the piedmont terrain, but at night it could be harrowing. Following Ellie's directions to the tee, Ben pulled into the half lit BuyMart parking lot nineteen minutes later, most of it surrounded by soaring loblolly pine trees, some reaching ninety feet tall. It was a cozy location even for a mega store the size of a football field.

The first thing Ben noticed was he could count the number of cars in the parking lot with one hand. In fact, there were only three, and his was one of them. Prior to moving, their local Miami BuyMart, open twenty-four hours a day, was always packed to the gills no matter what time it was. He'd seen his share of oddballs there too: extremely overweight women spilling out of their tiny spandex garments, men drinking beer concealed in brown paper bags, stupefied employees who couldn't direct you to a specific store product if their lives depended on it, you name it. Having spent most of his adult life in weird and wonderful south Florida, Ben mused that the only thing that would ever surprise him would be a person sprouting two heads.

As he got out of his car, Ben spotted a pair of twenty-something employees pushing shopping carts towards the entrance of the store. They were moving at a snails' pace. It was almost as if they were battling to see who could move the slowest.

"Good evening, gentlemen," said Ben as he walked by. The two employees barely raised their heads, mouths agape with a pair of blank stares.

People of BuyMart indeed, thought Ben as he entered the store. At least it wasn't one of those cavernous megastores like the one he used to frequent; this one was about a third smaller, almost intimate, if that was possible for such a mega store chain.

The shopping carts were in complete disarray, blocking most of the inside entrance. Ben zigzagged around them like an obstacle course before finding a lone cart up ahead. He grabbed the handle, only to find it sticky with some sort of drool.

I've been here a total of five seconds, and I'm already grossed out. He quickly doused his hands with hand sanitizer stationed over at the returns desk.

Ben took a deep breath and ambled forward without a cart this time. He passed multiple displays of sodas, cookies, and snack foods stacked precariously high like skyscrapers. Next, he eyed the produce section on the left, where the fruits and vegetables appeared way past their prime. Ben was taken aback; usually their produce department was exceptionally good – this one not so much. His mind was so preoccupied that he accidently bumped into a wall of a man sporting a stone-faced expression.

"Oh, my gosh! I'm so sorry sir." Ben apologized profusely, feeling like a complete idiot.

The employee glared down at Ben who must have been at least a foot shorter than him. The name 'Sven' was scribbled, Kindergarten-style, on the man's extra-large nametag in bold blue letters. He gawked at Ben for a moment, then said, "E-l-p?"

"Uh, yeah," replied Ben, being polite. "Could you please tell me where the pharmacy is?"

Sven did an about face, rotating in slow motion before pointing towards the back of the store. Ben followed as the sloth-like man began walking. He couldn't believe how sluggish the man was moving. Yearning to return home before sunrise, Ben darted ahead.

As he scanned the rest of the store, he noticed the handful of other employees moving at a turtle-like velocity. They all appeared like they were sleepwalking.

"Ah, there you are," he said, spotting the pharmacy section. "Nyquil, Nyquil, where art thou, Nyquil?"

He browsed the endless shelves, finally locating the cold and cough medicines. After picking up a bottle, Ben strolled around the corner shelf and snagged a carton of cherry lozenges for his minor sore throat. He then made a beeline for the chamomile tea before heading over to the cereal aisle. Like all BuyMart stores, the Pop-Tarts were situated just past the assortment of nutrition bars.

"Let's see, cinnamon frosted, strawberry frosted, cherry, chocolate chip, berry blast – all good flavors, but where is the elusive . . . ah there you are, chocolate-peanut butter. Yum!" Ben looked around slightly embarrassed. A thirty-eight-year old man shouldn't get that excited about a crummy pastry, but he was. Last stop, sardines. How *not* exciting, he mused.

As Ben rounded the corner, he heard a peculiar grunt. It was getting louder, now sounding more like multiple people. There was a sudden shriek, then silence, followed by a thump. Ben quickly hid behind a leaning tower of pasta display. He parted a couple of boxes of rigatoni to get a better look.

He watched as a pair of employees chomped down on a hapless shopper, a husky-framed man, possibly in his late fifties. Ben stood frozen, unable to move a muscle as a trail of blood flowed down the linoleum floor. He placed his hand over his mouth to keep from screaming. Around the corner, a short man with a buzz cut appeared huffing and puffing. He was a no-nonsense Ross Perot-looking type.

"Oh no, what the hell are you two doing?" he shouted. The man stormed over and threw down his clipboard. The two employees lowered their blood-stained faces, behaving almost like children being scolded by a parent.

The man appeared very upset, ranting as he looked up at the ceiling in full-fledged disgust. "After all the training, how could you do this?" He exhaled and addressed the two employees. "Rule number one: you never, ever eat the customers!" He picked up his clipboard off the floor, trying to regain his composure.

"You know what this means? The employees appeared in full shame mode, one almost weeping. "This is absolutely, positively gonna kill my promotion!"

He ran his left hand back and forth over his bristly, Astroturf-textured hair before storming towards a metal column. He gathered a deep breath before picking up the phone.

There was a screeching wall of feedback before the man's voice boomed over the loudspeaker. "I need a cleanup in aisle thirteen. I repeat, clean up in aisle thirteen."

He shook his head, gazing at the puddle of blood before calling again. "And bring the big mop." Putting the phone down, he looked at the employees. "You two, go get washed up, and try to move quickly."

Ben was trying to space the pasta boxes farther apart for a better look when, suddenly, the boxes came tumbling down. The employees turned to look at him. Ben almost wet his pants. He stared at the employees and offered up a harmless wave.

"Don't move," ordered the man.

"I'm not moving," replied Ben, still staring at the two killers, the lifeless, tubby body lying on the floor like a beached walrus.

The cleanup crew arrived; it was the two dolts from outside the store. One of the men began wrapping the dead person in a black plastic body bag while the other brandished a damp mop and began wiping up the mess.

Ben slowly regained his composure, the blood starting to flow again in his veins. "What the hell is going on here?"

The man walked towards him, sidestepping the stream of blood, almost skidding. "It's a tad complicated, sir."

"I've got time. Now tell me what the hell's going on here before I call the police."

The man hesitated. He took off his black-rimmed glasses, rubbed the bridge of his nose, and slipped them back on.

"This is strictly off the record, sir," said the man. "I guess I kinda owe you an explanation, but try and remember: loose lips drowns ships.

"I believe the word is, sinks," said Ben.

"I stand corrected," he replied, with a jovial grin. "Sometimes I get a mental block for words." He steered Ben away from the bloodstained aisle. "My name's Silva, Frank Silva, overnight manager. And yours?" The man extended his hand out. Ben, still in disbelief, shook it reluctantly. "Uh, Ben . . . Ben Gardner. My wife and I are new to the area. Just moved here from Miami."

"Terrific! Welcome to the Tar Heel State – hope you like pine trees,"

Silva glanced over at the two employees, instructing them to make everything clean as a whistle. Ben observed one of the employees attempting to whistle, but all that came out was spittle.

"Do you know why BuyMart is able to offer customers the best prices anywhere?"

"Everything's made in China?" replied Ben.

Silva snorted. "No, that's a fallacy, only partially true. Check out any other big-time retailer – we're no different than anyone else." Silva shook his head. "Well Ben, we're developing a unique workforce that doesn't require monetary fulfillment. They're dedicated, hardworking people, guaranteed to give their best effort a hundred percent of the time." He glanced at the subpar clean up attempt. "Well, mostly a hundred percent of the time." The man smirked then scratched his head.

"I'm sorry, what are you saying?" interrupted Ben, still dumbfounded.

"Due to our overnight crew's current 'status' on Earth, we're able to pay 'em in expired deli meats. They're quite content, usually." He frowned, then took a few steps forward, guiding Ben past the fallen pasta display. "They seem to prefer Boar's Head the most."

"Hold on," Ben interrupted. "I must be missing something here. You mean you feed your employees deli meat instead of paying them?"

"Yep. We save a butt-load of money. No salary, no health benefits, and as a result, we're able to pass those savings on to John Q. Shopper."

"How . . . I mean, what's wrong with them? They all seem so . . ."

"Lifeless?"

"That's about it," said Ben.

"Or maybe expired?" suggested Silva.

"I'm confused," said Ben, trying to put two and two together, but coming up with five instead of four. "You mean they're in some sort of hypnotized state?"

Silva giggled. "You're getting warmer."

"I am?" said Ben. "For Christ's sake, I don't even know what the hell I'm talking about!"

"You look like a decent guy, Ben, so I'll just spill the beans," said Silva. "We at BuyMart are implementing an exciting new employee program at select stores all across the country. One of the bigwigs in our advertising department even came up with a catchy acronym."

"What is it?"

"DED!"

"DED?"

"Yeppo," said Silva.

"And what exactly does that stand for?" asked Ben.

"Deceased Employee Directive," replied Silva, almost bursting in excitement. "I actually had a little input with the name. This unique 'workforce' is on the expired persuasion."

"Expired?" inquired Ben. "You mean like the deli meat you feed them? Hold on, we're not talking . . .No way."

"Yes way," grinned Silva.

The evening was turning into full bloom weirdness. Ben glared at the overnight manager, who was sporting a false smile that would rival a politician's. It was starting to dawn on Ben that the man was either completely insane, or . . .

"They don't call it the dead shift for nothing," Silva said. He shanked his brows up and down in patented Groucho Marx fashion. Ben corrected him — graveyard shift, not dead shift.

Silva started walking like Frankenstein's monster. "Hint, hint," he said with a wink. "The Z word."

"Zombies? You've hired actual zombies to work the night shift?"

"Bingo!"

"You can't be serious — can you?"

"Serious as a heart attack, my friend." Silva placed his arm around Ben's shoulders. "It's a pilot program we've developed over the last few of years, mostly at our rural locations or where we find a large congregation of weirdies so they can blend in easier. You said you moved here from Miami?"

"Yes," answered Ben, feeling like he'd stepped straight into a George A. Romero parody film.

"That was practically ground zero for the 'Z' program. Corporate thought it would be less conspicuous, especially in the Sunshine State. Betcha didn't even notice 'em where you shopped. Lots of oddballs there – but I guess you already know that."

All those times Ben went night shopping at BuyMart – and didn't even notice. He thought of himself as a fairly observant guy, but apparently not.

"This is extremely bizarre. I mean, undead workers? And what about . . . this?" Ben pointed at the victim, all ziplocked tight in a black body bag. "This is murder, plain and simple." Just then, the behemoth man walked up behind Ben, making him practically jump out of his skin.

"Ah, Sven," uttered Silva, who stood at least two feet shorter than Sven. Sven grunted. "Now this guy has been a prince of an employee. Won employee of the month the last three months in a row.

"Has he ever . . . killed anyone?" asked Ben, nervously. He figured at any moment the lumbering dead guy would go for his throat.

"Clean as a whistle," replied Silva. "Not one complaint or kill to report, if that's what you're speculating." He scratched his head. "Kinda ironic since he was a convicted murderer when he was alive."

"So, what are you going to do about this poor guy?" questioned Ben, his voice cracking at the absurdity of the situation. "This is plain murder."

"First off, it's a mishap, Ben; we call them mishaps. Now, I must admit things can get a bit dicey when dealing with our "formally" living shoppers. We sure as heck appreciated their loyalty and all, but life goes on."

"And how are you going to deal with . . . this?" Ben's voice elevating. "Your employees just chowed down him for God's sake!"

Silva gestured for Ben to calm down. "When situations like these arise, and again, let me emphasize that they are few and far between, we do our due-diligence. We do our best to make it look like a tragic accident. The truth is we have a lot invested here."

Ben shook his head, mouth agape. "So what you're really saying is an occasional fatality is just the price of doing business?"

"I guess you could put it that way," replied Silva. "Bottom line, young man, BuyMart will always do what it takes to offer our customers the best price – and that's my pledge to you."

"How noble."

"You're welcome."

"That was sarcasm," snapped Ben. "A person is dead, and you say it's a mishap? That's a bit frigid on your part, don't you think?"

"Look, I truly feel bad for the guy, but it *is* extremely uncommon," replied Silva. "In fact, I can't remember the last time we had a death. We spend months training our 'Z' staff. And they do a terrific job. The only real issue – besides on the very, very rare occasion when they dine on a customer, is their speed. These guys are slow as molasses."

"Sorry to burst your bubble, Frank, but they can barely communicate," said Ben. "And they're not very helpful."

"And the day shift employees are better?" snorted the manager, bursting out in full-fledged laughter. Ben shrugged, keeping a straight face. "But seriously."

Silva straightened his navy blue vest and looked at Ben square in the eyes. "Do you know we even hire speech therapists to work with 'em? Trust me, they're getting the hang of it. And I trust you don't mind paying pocket change for your Pop-Tarts."

Ben shrugged before glancing down at his watch. "Can I leave now? I gotta get back home to my wife. She needs her medicine."

"Look, you seem like a decent guy, and I know you won't say anything about tonight's mishap – or 'homicide' if that makes you feel any better. Besides, the whole story is so whacked no one's gonna believe you anyways. Tell you what: your shopping is on me this evening."

"Your generosity is overwhelming."

Silva guided Ben around a glob of blood. "Looks like our night crew missed a spot."

"Guess they need some more training," replied Ben dryly. He thanked Silva then proceeded to skip over the blotch of crimson red.

As he walked out the store, Ben noticed the nightshift employees following him, waving their stiff upper limbs in an attempt to wave good-bye. Ben jogged over to his car, hopped in, and sped out of the parking lot, not looking back. When he got home, Ellie was thankfully asleep, snoring like a Harley Davidson. He pondered calling the police, even dialing the phone before abruptly hanging up.

"That Silva guy is right," muttered Ben as he washed up in the bathroom. "No one is going to believe me." He changed into his pajamas and got into bed where he stared blankly at the ceiling for the next hour before finally falling asleep.

***

The next morning, Ben and Ellie sat at the kitchen table drinking coffee. Their daughter, Sophia, was getting dressed for school. The local morning news was on the small television anchored below one of the cabinets in the kitchen.

Ben was still uncertain if last night's events were nothing more than a bad dream or well-performed prank. He began to grin, thinking he may have been totally 'punked' last night, probably by his fellow teachers. What a sense of humor, he thought, the acting and special effects makeup top-notch.

"Thanks for getting the medicine, honey," said Ellie, still sniffling, but her cough subsiding. "I trust you didn't have a problem finding the store last night?"

"No problem, dear," said Ben, in better spirits as he took a hefty crescent-shaped bite from the chocolate peanut butter Pop-Tart. He sported a satisfied smile. "By the way, do you know why BuyMart is able to keep their prices so low?"

Ellie lifted her stuffy head, annoyed by the string of brazen car commercials on TV. "Everything's made in China?"

"Not everything," said Ben. They actually keep their prices low by hiring zombies to work the night shift. They pay them in deli scraps."

"You have a warped sense of humor, you know that?"

"Every joke has a half truth," replied Ben before polishing off the rest of the rectangular pastry. "Man, these are delicious."

"How sad," said Ellie.

"What, that I like Pop-Tarts?"

"No, Chubs, the news."

"What's that?" asked Ben, getting up to retrieve the orange juice from the refrigerator. He picked up the remote and kicked up the volume.

"A man identified as Carl Gottlieb, age fifty-seven, died late last night after he apparently plowed into a large tree, dying instantly." The news reporter added. "Police, however, are investigating the strange bite wounds located on the man's neck and arms."

Ben got chills, almost dropping his juice glass onto the tile floor. "Bite marks? Uh, probably just from a bear or mountain lion."

"Or maybe there are flesh-eating zombies lurking in the deep, dark forests of North Carolina," replied Ellie in a ghoulish fashion. "How's that for warped?"

Ben plopped another Pop-Tart into the toaster. "The truth is stranger than fiction."

The Aquarium

Marineworld, one of the first ever-created aquariums of its kind way back in mid-twentieth century Florida, stood vacant, succumbing to time and the newer, state-of-the-art models. Seventy years is a long time in the entertainment business to be the top dog, or in this case, the top dogfish. It was a good while it lasted.

The storied aquarium enthralled thousands of visitors of all ages, eager to experience the undersea world of Jacques Cousteau up close and personal. There were dangerous sharks, slippery seals, and a myriad of tropical fish, all visible through three-inch thick walls of tempered glass. Even Hollywood got in the act, using the facility to shoot B-horror movies.

But now, the only things remaining were rust covered railings, crumbling cement walls, and the ghostly cheers of children soaking in decades of dolphin shows.

At least two locals still appreciated it.

"You brought the spray paint, right?" Daniel Lutz blurted out to his friend, Seth Brogan, as they approached the abandoned aquarium on foot at half past midnight. Daniel was built like a treasure chest: simple, stocky, and rounded. He always wore the same big-tongued Rolling Stones concert t-shirt, complete with baggy olive drab shorts that went past his knees.

With his scraggly facial hair, he appeared like some sort of Neanderthal groupie.

"Keep it in your pants, dill weed," Seth answered, a former high school football star now full-time slacker at age nineteen. "See? I got it right here: red, white, and blue. Very patriotic don't you think?" Independence Day was only a week away, but he could read his friend's disappointment. "Hey, it seemed appropriate."

"Idiotic is more like it," Daniel replied. "Where the hell are the neon colors? No orange or green in that bag? That's what gets us noticed, dipshit!"

The two soon-to-be-twenty-year-olds thought of themselves as budding graffiti artists, but more closely resembled bored, middle class burnouts. They had taken a fancy to defacing the vacant aquarium, filled with ungroomed palm trees and tallish weeds. The duo generally preferred spray-painting fat rounded letters around the crumbling facility like some sort of Botero-inspired alphabet. A week before, Daniel had broken out his cartooning prowess with a seven-foot neon orange Jaws face accented with a big fat dube hanging from the corner of its crescent-shaped mouth.

Tonight though, Daniel was feeling antsy and in an investigative mood. He began scavenging around the old exhibit hall building hoping to find a left-over souvenir before venturing outside near the dried-up waist-high touch tanks. From the corner of his eye he spotted the maintenance building walled in by unkempt vegetation.

He tracked the overgrown gravel walkway like a zealous hound dog, following the meandering pathway through and around palm trees, when he suddenly tripped over a low-slung line of barbed wire. He didn't even notice the bold lettered metal 'Keep Out' sign he'd just stumbled over.

"Son of a bitch," he shouted, falling face first onto a gathering of dead, dry, hardened royal palm fronds. He would've much preferred landing in soft autumn leaves piled high as baled hay. Sometimes he really wished his parents hadn't moved away from the Buckeye State.

"What's up?" Seth called out. He was putting the finishing touches on a patriotic portrait of Homer J. Simpson, about the only thing he could really draw well. He placed the spray cans in the plastic BuyMart bag and jogged over, following his friend's voice down the worn path.

"Over here," Daniel called out as he brushed himself off. He called out again, this time with more urgency like he'd discovered a hidden treasure. He waved Seth over with the flashlight, pointing it at the seven-foot high wooded fence. "This could be very interesting."

"Cool . . . but what's with the warning signs?" asked Seth, observing the two posted at each corner of the rotted out wooden fence.

Daniel stood on top of a sawed-off palm tree stump. "Shit, that sign is probably a hundred years old. More importantly, I'm gonna need your physical expertise." Daniel flashed a very Grinchian grin.

At six-foot-three, Seth was Frankenstein strong, enough to tear the whole fence down to the ground with his bare hands. The ex-jock stepped forward, wrapped his meaty fingers on the top of the fence and ripped off a slat. He repeated the primeval process six more times before peering through the opening.

Daniel hopped down off the stump before poking his chubby face through the opening. "Hey, there's a chain link fence behind this one and some sort of building."

"Fucking-A, I got a splinter," winced Seth as he tried to remove it. "Uh, what'd you say?" The stout teen finally took a gander at the double fenced barricade. "The aquarium people musta forgot something in there – maybe it's valuable."

Both young men perked up. Seth especially, whose greedy imagination brimmed with dollar signs. He was dead broke, and his parents were tired of flushing money down the toilet for their non-working leech of a son.

Seth dropped the bag of spray paint cans and didn't bother to pick it up. He was too excited. "Yeah, who knows what lurks beyond these walls!"

"You can be creepy sometimes, you know that?" said Daniel

The two managed to squeeze through the wood fence opening then greeted the chain link variety, the door secured with an old model heavy-duty padlock the size of a baseball. Seth inspected the device. On the back of the lock was a faded Universal Studio logo. The image didn't register as he pulled with all his strength to open it.

"Crap. Looks like we'll have to climb it," said Seth, slamming the lock against the rusted chain link fence.

"It's doesn't look too bad, maybe ten feet tops," said Daniel confidently. "I'll lend you a hand." Daniel was horrible at climbing anything. He quickly experienced an elementary school flashback where in gym class he failed to climb the fitness rope. All he could remember was his whole class laughing at him. He was forever nicknamed 'Butterball.'

"Hey, why me first?" replied Seth. He looked at his friend; he knew what was coming next.

"Chicken, are we?" squawked Daniel.

Seth snarled, "Alright, but I get sixty percent of what's in there, you hear me?"

Daniel nodded, a bit surprised by his friend's sudden assertiveness. He was fairly certain, actually one-hundred percent certain, that Seth could pound him into the ground like a Jobe's tree spike anytime he wanted too, so he knew when to rein in the verbal barbs. "Here, take the flashlight with you."

Seth grabbed the yellow object from Daniel's hand and placed the safety band around his wrist. The limber teen scaled the fence like a circus monkey, already halfway down the other side in a minute before dropping the last four feet onto a bunch of tall, standing weeds. There were scattered empty beer cans, a couple even had the old-style pull-tabs, along with an assortment of fast food trash. He spotted an old movie poster on the door, the watermarked image of a curvaceous woman, along with a weird-shaped face.

The rest of the walls had miscellaneous deep groove marks intertwined with the peeling sky blue paint. Seth paused for a moment, thinking that was rather peculiar. He was suddenly hit with an all-encompassing body chill, but it didn't last long. The thought of money, and lots of it, evaporated those feelings in a heartbeat. He surveyed the grounds before heading towards the rotted locked door. It looked like the place hadn't been visited in half a century.

Seth squinted his eyes in deep concentration at the door like a blitzing linebacker ready to tee off on a receiver running a crossing route. He took a few steps back, crouched down in a battering ram position, and smacked into the door straight on with his still muscular shoulder, busting it wide open.

The momentum carried him inside into a dank room. As Seth stood up, he took in a deep breath and gagged. "Ugh." It smelled stale, like a junked refrigerator that hadn't been opened in years. The cement floor was partially carpeted with moist, putting, green-shaded moss. His heavy body weight created an echo with each step he took.

"Hey, there's a pool in here; decent size too."

"What does it look like?" asked Daniel.

"It's big and round, but I can't see anything in the water," answered Seth. "It's all covered in green algae"

"Who knows, maybe there's a rare species of fish in there," Daniel called out.

"Are you coming or not?" asked Seth, looking back at his friend. "This is really, really cool."

Seth waved away a few cobwebs and strolled over to the pool. He focused the light beam as he paced around the surrounding four-foot high cement barrier wall like an archeologist discovering some ancient temple. The strange body of water was still as death. An indistinguishable growth drooped along the cement texture. The lone circular pool, no more than fifteen feet in circumference, remained unspoiled. It was filled to the brim with stagnant water, a thick film of bottle green algae coating the surface. Moonlight shined through the yellowed rectangular skylight, providing the young man with additional visibility.

"Hey, I see bubbles. You gotta get over here!"

"I'm trying, I'm trying," snapped Daniel. His blunt-nosed black boots made it impossible to get a grip inside the tight chain link spaces.

"Try taking your boots off; you'll get better footing," suggested Seth. Daniel shrugged his shoulders like he should have come up with the idea himself. The ground was damp, and he wasn't keen on dirtying up his white tube socks but figured if his friend could climb it, so could he.

"I'm on my way," announced Daniel, like he was doing something monumental. "Not too bad, so far." The fence rattled and squeaked as he prodded his heavy frame upward ever so slowly.

Seth continued to circle the pool, hoping to spot anything living in the murky goop. He changed gears and aimed the flashlight on the cement floor. He spotted cigarette butts and more empty beer cans – some unopened, littered along the cement floor.

"Hey, other people must a been here."

He noticed a jagged-shaped opening on the opposite end of the structure where someone had smashed through. He picked up one of the full cans of beer, sniffing it.

"Dude, this beer ain't too old." Seth wiped the top off on his t-shirt then popped the top. Beer shot out everywhere before subsiding. He poured some in his mouth, not wanting to place his lips on the can. He quickly spat it out. "Ugh, man this beer is skunked supreme!"

"I coulda told you that, pumpkin nuts," chortled Daniel, still struggling with his inner climbing demons.

"Come on Heavy D, get moving," encouraged Seth, as he combed the surroundings like a behemoth sleuth looking for clues.

"Almost there."

Seth peered over the edge, the cheap dollar store flashlight fading already. He tapped it against the palm of his hand. Presto, bright beam. There, half hidden under a sheet of rotting cardboard he picked up a foot-long stick, clutching the nub on the end. Seth stroked the surface of the water, brushing away the coated layer of slime. He felt a tickling sensation. Something didn't feel right.

"What the fuck?" Seth ran the beam of light down the stick. "

It was a human bone, ants parading up and down his fingers as they nibbled away on the remaining bits of flesh. He tossed it away as his foot knocked into something heavy. The object bowled over, banking off the cement wall. His heart racing, Seth reluctantly pointed the flashlight beam down to the ground. He nearly puked at the sight of a half decomposed human skull. He could just make out the partial straight black ponytail with a pink ribbon still in tow. He trembled, doubling over in horror. "Holy shit," he uttered in a weak, high-pitched tone under his breath.

Seth glanced back at the pool and was suddenly mesmerized by slight movement in the thick soup.

The moonlight above shone on the surface like a stage light. His eyes followed a stream of bubbles heading in his direction. He inched closer to the edge of the pool and gazed as hard as he could through the algae but couldn't decipher much. There, a pale shape slowly emerged through the murkiness – closer and closer, like a revealing magic eight ball. Seth gazed harder.

It appeared as a horrific reflection, humanesque but with reptilian features. The face had a textured, hunter-green appearance, tapered snout, eyes sinister and slanted, and a mouth lined with savage piranha sharp teeth. Seth's wide eyes were way ahead of his words. He didn't have time to scream. The shape lunged out of the water and chomped down on Seth's jugular, dragging him underwater in an instant. The sudden fury calmed in seconds.

"Here's Johnny," yelled Daniel, finally scaling the chained metal fortress, jumping down to the ground with a thud. "Seth?"

He marched through the open doorway and spotted the flashlight on the damp floor. He looked around pensively then picked it up. He pointed it around the room: nothing. From the corner of his eye he noticed a faint ripple in the water.

"Hey Seth," he called out, wondered if his friend had fallen in, or maybe took off instead, leaving him there alone. Always a practical joker.

"Okay, time to jump out and scare me," called Daniel as he strolled over to the pool. The water had a peculiar, brick red hue, almost rust colored; he could have sworn his friend said the water looked green. As he watched, Seth's body suddenly rose to the surface, bloody and mangled. Half his face torn off. Daniel let out a horrified scream, frozen in disbelief as the creature emerged from the water and shoved the tattered body back underwater. He finally caught his breath and made a mad scramble for the chain link fence. He flung his outstretched hands upwards in desperation, grasping the rattling thin metal and trying to escape. He shouted at the top of his lungs. "Help me, anyone! Help!"

The creature, with its plated body and scaly limbs, stood upright, standing nearly seven feet tall. There was a rusted shackle attached to its right ankle and a heavy-linked chain that led back to the deep center of the pool. Whatever it was, it was meant to stay hidden. The creature snarled, unable to move any closer.

Daniel, approaching the top of the fence, quickly glanced back and saw the creature stuck near the pool. A monstrous sense of relief filled him. He laughed hysterically then flashed his sausage-like middle finger towards the beast. He proceeded to fire off a slew of expletives ending with an elegant, "Fuck you, gill weed."

The creature howled. It began to tug violently at the chain. One of the rusted links snapped. Its yellow eyes sensed freedom as it lunged over towards Daniel. The young man slipped momentarily but managed to hoist himself again to the top of the fence. He was almost free and clear . . . almost.

The creature, utilizing its webbed claws, easily scaled the fence like a spider. It latched onto Daniel's bowling-pin thick calf muscle and tore into it, shearing the flesh to the bone. Blood cascaded from the shredded muscle. The creature climbed higher, grasping its claws around Daniel's waist. It pried him off the fence as both plummeted to the hard cement floor. The creature twisted like a fighting alligator, pinning him to the floor. The last thing Daniel experienced was the creature's open maw targeting his throat.

In the blink of an eye, Daniel was dead. The creature plunged its blackened claws deep into Daniels' upper torso and dragged him to the side of the pool. It slithered back into the water, victim in tow, barely creating a ripple.

Pleased to Eat You

"I am famished," proclaimed Bob Unger, eager to chow down with his wife, Helen, and their two children as they patiently waited to be seated at the restaurant.

"Well, you've come to the right place," replied the spunky brunette hostess, overhearing Unger, a hefty man sporting slightly wrinkled khaki pants and a bright green sweater. The Unger family were regulars at the popular Home Body Buffet, dining there weekly.

"This way, folks," said the waitress.

The four were seated at their regular table stationed within proximity to the expansive buffet spread for easy access. Bob and his twelve-year-old son Toby were chomping at the bit.

"Okay kids, you know the drill: get your plates, silverware, and lots of napkins," said Helen, plumpish and pleasant in her flowery yellow house dress. "And Toby, absolutely no cutting in line. Last time was embarrassing, jumping in front of that old woman, just for another thigh!"

"All right, all right, I promise – sheesh," replied Toby, a near replica of his old man.

"And Alice, please don't be so finicky this time," added Helen, addressing her slender daughter. "You father spends a pretty penny to come here."

"Yes, Mommy dearest," replied Alice, a surly high school honors student, slender and smart; the black sheep of the family.

Bob and Toby salivated as they circled the large buffet table like hungry sharks. Helen patiently waited her turn. Alice meanwhile made a beeline for the vacant salad bar and picked freely.

"Ooh, look, fresh CEO," observed Bob. "Musta got 'em today from the big city."

Helen passed, preferring a sample of sports athletes – something lean and trim. She'd been dying to lose twenty pounds, even taking a stab at the Atkins diet.

"But at some point, you run out of Atkins's," Bob liked to quip. He loved that line, blurting out in laughter and snorting like a pig.

Bob sauntered over to the Catch of the Day but suddenly cringed. "Politicians? Man, oh man, this joint is scraping the bottom of the barrel. Toby, stay away from that or you'll be sitting on the can for a week. I wouldn't eat 'em if they were the last people on earth."

Alice walked past her family carrying two small plates: one filled with cut melon, apples, and pears; the other a tossed salad with vinaigrette dressing. All her friends had the same palate, but her parents always insisted on adding finger food to her meals.

Helen noticed her daughter's sparse plate. "Alice dear, you need to eat more. At least try the librarian – they're low-calorie."

"Librarian?" laughed Bob. "Hell, why don't you just gnaw on a tree limb for God's sake?" Mr. Unger was in fine comedic form. A full-time professional funnyman, Unger literally killed his audience.

"Maybe if you'd stop chomping down on those slow-moving BuyMart types, you wouldn't be so overweight," said Alice.

"Hey, I'm in good shape," replied Bob as he peeked down at his bulbous frame. "Well, maybe not."

After fixing his plate, Bob turned to his son, still picking and choosing. "I wanna test out a new joke – actually it's an old joke but with a fresh new punchline."

Toby shrugged, fancying to load up his Frisbee-sized plate first. "Okay, Pops, spill your guts."

Bob laughed. "Hey, I like that; mind if I use it tomorrow night at the *'Fryers'* Club?"

"Sure, why not," replied Toby.

"Okay. A horse trots into a bar and the bartender says, Hey, why the long face?"

Toby rolled his eyes. "That's it?" Usually his dad was much funnier, or so he'd heard.

"Hold your horses, kid, I'm not done yet," smirked Bob. "Here's the new and improved punchline."

"Come on Dad," whined Toby, his stomach growling in hunger. "I wanna eat."

"So, the horse replies, 'Cause my wife was just turned into glue!" Bob howled in laughter; Toby, not so much. A single mother, properly dressed, gasped. "Sir, that was in absolutely poor taste!" She proceeded to select a healthy-looking forearm for her son and stormed off.

Noticing the captive audience, the always effervescent Bob brought out his home run material. "Hey folks, you know why cannibals don't eat clowns? 'Cause they taste funny! Haaaaa!" The whole place erupted in groans, even the waitresses.

"Why does he have to do that lame joke all the time; it's so embarrassing," quipped Alice as she and her mom sat down at the table.

"You've only experienced it for a few years, dear. Try twenty for me," shrugged Helen.

Bob and Toby walked over with filled plates and supersized sodas and joined the family at the table. Alice dined on her salad and fruit, contented. Toby quickly dug into his plateful of organs. Helen gnawed on forearms and finger food while Bob feasted on shanks of community college professor, hoping it would make him smarter.

Alice finished up her meal first, placing the napkin over her plate. She winced as her family gorged themselves. She sighed. "You know it never use to be this way. People eating people. Humans used to have diverse diets rich in fruits, grains, vegetables, fish, and meats.

"That was over a hundred years ago dear," said Helen, taking a sip of sweetened iced tea. "You should know from history – how viruses wiped out the entire food supply on Earth. And the fish, they got smart and swam into deeper waters, unable to be caught. In desperation, people turned on each other, and in due time, we liked it."

"I read that fat people were the first to go – those couch potatoes never had a chance," said Bob.

"And you could be next," said Alice. "You know eating healthy won't kill you but eating unhealthy will."

"That was so wise," said Helen, adding a pinch more salt to her forearm.

Bob belched, apologizing quickly as he gazed at his mammoth plate of guts. "You're right Alice, I really gotta do better or I'll be next."

"I read somewhere that people use to eat barbecued ribs . . . from pigs!" added Helen.

"What's a pig?" asked Toby, his face a bloody mess.

Alice was about to utter something unflattering under her breath but refrained. "All of you need to eat like me. Or else."

"And what, should I start grazing on the front lawn?" joked Bob. "Maybe pour some thousand-island dressing and sprinkle a few croutons on our fine Kentucky bluegrass?"

"Don't be ridiculous," jabbed Helen. "Our daughter is the bright bulb in the family; we should listen more."

"Well, I for one am permanently swearing off people!" boasted Alice. Mr. and Mrs. Unger gasped, hoping no one else overheard their daughter.

"Sorry folks, she's is a bit under the weather," said Helen, sporting a half-hearted smile.

Alice took out a small plastic container from her cute panda shaped backpack and stealthily handed it to her dad. "Here, you need to try this instead."

Bob pried it open, grimacing at the unrecognizable object. It had a crusty texture and was still warm. "What the heck is it?"

"Take a bite," said Alice, cautioning her dad to be discreet. "You're not scared, are you?"

"I'm not scared of nothing, except when your mother gets really upset at me," mused Bob. He paused, eying his daughter. "Okay, okay, I'll try it."

Glancing around at the other diners, Bob secretly removed the food item from the container and bit into it. His eyes lit up like a Christmas tree in approval and continued munching. "Wow! What is this?"

"It's called a chicken leg," said Alice. "My friends and I were able to recreate a wide range of farm animals. My best friend's dad is a brilliant research scientist who helped us. We've got pigs, cows, goats, even ducks! They're all secretly stored at the abandon barn behind my friend's house."

"I think I'm in love with chicken," drooled Bob. "You got any more?"

"Lots more," said Alice." We're going to expand the project so we don't have to eat humans anymore. Aren't you getting tired of chasing down the postal worker for breakfast, or preying on my teachers? We can't find a decent substitute anymore. And besides, it's really messy too."

"Yeah, I suppose so," replied Bob. "You really think we can all survive on this?" He ogled the chicken bone, cleanly stripped of all the meat. "I'm missing it already."

"Oh yeah," Alice replied emphatically. Toby was barely paying attention, munching down on liver.

"Well, good for you!" said Helen, proud of her brainiac daughter. "Always the thinker." Alice smiled.

"Well, let's blow this popsicle stand and eat more chicken!" boasted Bob. After everyone had washed up, he paid the bill and the family of four headed outside.

Bob took in a deep breath of air and exhaled. "I say we go topless tonight," he proposed, always eager to show off his crimson red Lincoln Continental convertible.

"Maybe we shouldn't," said Alice.

"Ah, it's perfect out tonight, and besides, I feel like we've all been reborn, or something to that effect, said Bob. "As of this moment, the Unger family is swearing off people!"

Bob took out his car keys, dangling them in from of Alice. "I know you've been itching to drive the land yacht."

"Um, okay," smiled Alice.

The four got in with Alice at the helm. She adjusted the seat, properly checked the mirrors and buckled up. Navigating out of the parking lot, she drove blissfully around the scenic town, enjoying the crisp spring evening air, music blaring. She slowed down as the traffic light signal turned red.

"You're doing really great, kid," said Bob, sitting in the front passenger seat. He turned to Helen sitting in the back seat with Toby. He barely had time to scream.

A gang of famished cannibal thugs attacked the Ungers, devouring them in mere seconds like a school-full of ravenous piranhas.

They left nothing but the bones.

Pumpkin and Vine

An obsidian black Mercedes G-Class SUV sped along a rustic backroad, devoid of landmarks or street signs of any kind. For the male occupants, it had been a hectic workweek doling out pain and misery to the competition. A relaxing weekend getaway was in order by the wives. But the moment, they were totally lost.

"Fucking GPS, piece of shit," uttered Tommy Casanova, not exactly savoring the bone-jarring, off-road experience. "Where the hell are we?"

"We'll find the bed and breakfast, Honey," said Maria, his wife of eight years. "The problem is you gotta stop being so . . . Oh my God, Tommy. Pull over, pull over!" squawked Maria, grabbing her husband's rock-solid shoulder. The woman's grating Long Island accent, thick and rich, was headache inducing.

He slammed on the brakes, making an abrupt right-hand turn up an unkempt, weed-filtered gravel driveway. Tommy parked the car under a soaring, lifeless tree where a rotted-out birdhouse dangled from a heavy branch. The dented black mailbox stood with the name "Rey" finger-painted in bold white letters.

His wife, in her mid-thirties, short, curvy, with long black hair and heels so lengthy they would keep her safe in floodwater, shot out of the car and stampeded over to the picket fence surrounding the pumpkin patch like a graceless show horse, a sea of gold jewelry slinking up and down her skinny wrists. Mikey, Tommy's cousin, and his wife Ginger, got out and stretched their limbs.

"I gotta have two of those; my nieces Zoe and Chloe will go gaga!" declared Maria. She gazed around the property. Seeing no one, she called out. "Hello? Anyone here?"

Her husband begrudgingly got out of the car, a hulking bowling ball of a man who cared about country life about as much as eating Chef Boyardee. He heard noises coming from the dilapidated red-washed barn. A tall man, possibly early fifties, was hunched over, tinkering on a vintage green tractor.

Maria, spotting the man from afar, called out. "Hey Mister, I wanna buy your pumpkins."

The man, tall and slender with straw-like silver blond hair, a living, breathing fusion of Andy Warhol and Clint Eastwood, wore washed out blue jeans with a black-and-red checkered flannel shirt. He gritted his teeth as he tossed the rag aside and stalked over. His hazel eyes perked up, yet his cold, wrinkle-free face, almost doll-like in complexion, remained stoic. He stalked over to the unwanted people, clutching his wrought-iron pitchfork. The two-foot long tines stuck out like viper fangs.

"Get out now," he said, his voice coming out in a resonating, sandpaper rough tone. "Can't you read? It says, 'No Trespassing'!"

"Huh?" Maria turned her head as she chomped away on wads of neon pink bubble gum. She was totally enthralled by the pumpkin patch, a sweeping field of tangled vines that encroached Mr. Rey's decrepit two-story farmhouse like barbed wire. "I couldn't hear you. What'd you say?

Mr. Rey moved closer. "Get off my property."

"Come on, Mister," whined Maria, a technique that had produced plenty of jewelry from Tommy. "I gotta get two of your gorgeous red pumpkins. They're for my nieces!" Maria explored her Samsonite-sized Prada brand white leather purse and pulled out a crisp fifty-dollar bill. Her husband leaned against his Benz, arms crossed and completely bored. Mikey and Ginger milled around the white picket fence fortressing the pumpkin patch.

"They're not for sale. Now get off my property or I will kill you!"

The woman giggled, turning to her husband in mock horror. "Tommy, he says he wants to kill me!"

"Really? Do us all a favor, old man," replied her husband, smirking.

"Tommy," said Maria, drawing out her husband's name in a torturous inflection.

Tommy was bored as snot and just wanted to get back to the Queens, but he had promised his wife a relaxing country weekend. He uncrossed his arms and rolled up his sweater sleeves and sauntered over to Mr. Rey, who towered over the brawny man by nearly a foot.

"Hey Farmer Brown," said Tommy. He heard his cousin, Mikey snicker. "Whad'ya say you let us buy a couple of your pumpkins and we'll be on our way."

"They are not for sale. Now leave or I will kill you."

"Sounds pretty harsh coming from a sheep shagger," grinned Tommy, his Mafioso wrath simmering. "And if you really threatened my wife, I may need to rectify the situation, you catch my drift?" Mikey and Ginger froze. Tommy Casanova was a mob pro and had no problem 'taking care of people.' Idle threats were not part of his vernacular.

He stepped closer to the tall man until he stood no more than six inches away. "I'm talking to you, doll face," said Tommy, reaching the boiling point.

He pointed his sausage-link index finger in the man's face, almost touching his nose. He once joked he had probably broken every bone in his hands by rearranging many a facial structure. "Well?"

Mr. Rey returned a cold stare, his thin grayish lips barely visible. Tommy's angered brow formed a wrinkled V-shape. He inched closer. His finger touched the tip of Mr. Rey's nose.

That's when all hell broke loose.

In a split second, the farmer took his enormous left hand and grabbed Tommy by the throat, lifting him off the ground. Mr. Rey's eyes burned in guttural hate.

"Holy shit," shouted Mikey, a near physical replica of his cousin but four years younger and twenty pounds heavier.

"Tommy!" screamed Maria hysterically. "It's just pumpkins, you ass face."

Mr. Rey threw Tommy onto the trampled grass and leaves. Tommy got back up and reached for the knife tucked in his coat pocket. Before he could extend his arm, Mr. Rey knocked it out of his hand with a kick then pointed the pitchfork tines directly at Tommy's throat. One of the knife-sharp tips nicked the skin just below Tommy's Adam's apple, drawing a trickle of blood.

"Hey, let's just remain calm, shall we?" said Mikey as he shuffled over to help his cousin off the ground and straighten Tommy's ruffled sweater. Tommy swatted Mikey's arms away, now full of rage.

"I'd kill you, you son of a bitch right here and now, but as a rule, I don't kill no one with my wife present."

"Oh, that's so sweet," said Maria as she hugged Tommy's arm.

"For the last time, get off of my property – now!" Mr. Rey shouted, with more graveled venom in his voice. Tommy retrieved his knife before storming back to the car.

"You picked the wrong person to mess with, psycho!" bellowed Tommy, as he stepped into his car, bumping his head as he got in.

"Enough, honey, let just get out of here!" said Maria.

Tommy floored the gas, leaving a spray of gravel and dust from the weathered driveway. As they sped away, Tommy whispered to his cousin sitting in the front passenger seat. "We're coming back here tonight to finish this, you hear me?" Mikey paused then nodded in agreement.

***

Halloween night reached half past eleven, temperatures hovering in the mid-forties. After a subpar Italian dinner and tasteless bottle of domestic red wine at the bed and breakfast, both men left their spouses in blissful, cozy, coastal town sleep.

"Is this really necessary?" asked Mikey, a bit drunk from all the wine. "I was gettin' ready to watch *Sports Center*."

"Zip it, linguini spine," answered Tommy. "That freak . . . no one grabs my fucking throat and lives! You should know that by now."

"Yeah, you're right Tommy," replied Mikey. "Strong dude, huh?"

Tommy stared straight ahead, "Yeah."

Mikey glanced over at Tommy. He'd never seen his cousin unnerved like that before, not even before his wedding day or the time he had to whack a backstabbing relative. Tommy turned the lights off as they approached the dilapidated farmhouse, stopping thirty yards short of the uphill driveway. He parked under a line of leafless oak trees, their limbs reaching out like invading monsters.

"If any birds crap on your car, I'll roast these trees personally for you," bragged Mikey. The two closed the car doors; Mikey's a bit too loud —Tommy shot him an icy stare. Tommy shut the drivers' side door then gave it a gentle bump with his hip.

"You don't broadcast when you're about to whack someone, nimrod," scolded Tommy. "Get the gas can in the trunk – you got your lighter, I presume?"

"You're asking me if I have a lighter?" replied Mikey. Mikey displayed his five-figure, custom-made gold lighter in his right hand, a book of matches from the bed and breakfast in his left. "Don't leave home without 'em."

Mikey was nicknamed "The Torch" by his mob buddies and always carried his trusty 18-karat gold lighter in his pocket and a hefty five-gallon metal gasoline can in the back of his custom-painted, glittering bronze Cadillac Escalade.

Tommy grinned. "Always prepared, like a good boy scout."

The two men were clad in the same attire they had worn earlier for dinner, including their expensive, white Italian dress shoes. They hiked up the leaf-covered incline, both slipping in the damp earth.

The house stood fifty yards away. The front porch light was on, along with a lone room upstairs. Vultures sat perched on the naked trees circling the property, none making a sound. The large barn doors partially open.

"Maybe he's in there? All that hay will make this a cinch," said Mikey. The moist ground squished with every step the two made.

"Ready to jump it?" asked Mikey, as they approached the deteriorating picket fence.

"Hell no," replied Tommy. He quietly pried the pointed slats from the rickety barrier with his bare hands, creating plenty of space. "After you."

The two hunched down as they approached the pumpkin patch. The boundless rope of vines encompassed the whole back yard like a bowl of spaghetti. "Maybe we'll see the Great Pumpkin tonight?" joked Mikey.

"Shut up," snapped Tommy. "I am in no joking mood."

"Look at these things?" gulped Mikey, staring at the sea of red pumpkins, "I mean, they all look a little too, you know, perfect, don't they?"

"Like that guy's face," answered Tommy, gritting his teeth.

The two followed the trail of vines leaning to the back yard. The far reaches were filled with trees, mostly pines and maples. As they approached a lone apple tree, the two squashed and slipped on the rotted fruit. Tommy caught himself, but Mikey took a tumble, landing straight on his back. The gasoline can he was carrying nearly fell smack dab on his head.

"What are you, the Three Stooges or something?" said Tommy. "Enough of the slapstick."

"Sorry, sorry," replied Mikey, rubbing his lower back.

A thick congregation of pumpkin vines seemed to venture out from a solitary location about thirty yards from the back of the house, an area already cluttered by rusted out farm equipment. There was a rotting smell, like dead animals.

"I know in our line of work we don't visit pumpkin patches too often, but jeeze, this place smells like . . . where we 'dump the bodies,' you know what I mean?" said Mikey, making air quotation marks with his fingers.

"Yeah," Tommy concurred.

The two men tiptoed between the foliage. Tommy reached for his pen flashlight and bent down to touch one of the pumpkins. "You know this feels weird," he said, rubbing his fingertips together, "They're soft like . . . skin, or something." His cousin reached down and did the same.

Mikey flicked out a silver six-inch folding knife from his back pocket and placed the blade under a hearty vine, thick and flexible like rope. "I can't cut it."

"My sentiments exactly," replied Tommy. "Gimme that!"

Tommy used the knife and attempted to cut through the pumpkin vine. "See, I told you," said Mikey, watching his cousin struggle. "I'm tellin' you, this whole thing is getting strange – like *Twilight Zone* strange."

"Don't get stupid," said Tommy, annoyed. "Maybe we just need to try something different. Here, hold the goddamn flashlight."

"What are you gonna do?" questioned Mikey.

Tommy bent down on one knee like he was going to propose to the volleyball-sized plump, red pumpkin. Studying it for a moment, the mobster gripped the knife in his right hand and poked the tip of the blade into the pumpkin's smooth surface. A minuscule drop of red fluid leaked out like a teardrop.

"Juicy, ain't it?" observed Mikey. "Hold on, pumpkins aren't –"

Tommy placed the blade in the same spot, but this time, plunged the blade straight into the pumpkin's flesh. Blood squirted from the wound as the impaled shape let out a minuscule, high-pitched cry.

"What the hell was that?" yelled Mikey, as he looked over at Tommy, his face now painted with blood. "Oh, this is messed up; let's get the hell out of here!"

Getting to his feet, Tommy reached into his back pocket for a handkerchief to wipe the liquid off his face. He then kicked the pumpkin, making a dent, but hurt his foot in the process, his shoe now sponged in crimson.

"Let's torch this fucking dump, now," growled Tommy.

Suddenly, the backscreen door creaked opened with Mr. Rey brandishing a double-barrel shotgun. The tall man stared at his field of prized red pumpkins. A pair of vultures took off from a branch just above the two men who were lying flat on their stomachs.

Mr. Rey fired, blowing both birds out of the sky. Their remnants fell on top of the two men. The decapitated head of one of the birds landed a foot away from Mikey's peering eyes, still twitching. He almost barfed on the spot. Mr. Rey stood as still as one of his ghoulishly posted scarecrows before finally going back inside.

Tommy got to his knees and whispered to his cousin. "Time to barbeque this son of a bitch and take out the pumpkin patch with it."

The two men stood up, but Tommy stepped on something solid near the base of the pumpkin vines. He felt a wood board under his feet, partially covered by leaves and dead grass. Tommy shone his flashlight, revealing two rusted metal handles on the two four-by-eight-foot wood planks. He waved his cousin over. "Maybe it's a trap door that leads to his house," surmised Mikey.

The weight of the two men broke the wood, throwing them down into a deep 10-foot pit. They were in total darkness.

"Tommy, can you hear me?" Mikey called out.

"Oh my God, what the hell is this?" cried Tommy. The two men tried to stand up, but the footing was cumbersome – hard and uneven but soft in spots. The smell was rancid and nauseating.

Tommy fumbled for his flash light, the small beam partially hidden under something moist. He picked it up and pointed it at his cousin. Directly behind him and all around were piles of rotting corpses in various stages of decay. The smell was unbearable. Mikey couldn't hold in the nausea any longer, vomiting in a corner. Tommy frantically waved the flashlight back and forth.

A forest of thick celery-green roots dropped down like paratroopers from the hole above and through the dirt; it was everywhere. Tommy dragged the flashlight beam from top to bottom. Horrified, he saw the ends of the roots burrowing into the scattered dead bodies, some very recent.

"Oh my God," said Mikey, his mouth agape. Tommy looked closer at the translucent roots, blood now flowing upward into . . .

"Those pumpkins," Tommy uttered. "Those fucking pumpkins are living off the blood of people. We gotta get the hell out of here!"

The roots starting swaying back and forth. They began to wrap around the arms of the two men.

"Augh! My knife, where's my goddamn knife?" screamed Mikey. One particular root reached into Tommy's ear. He seized it with his bare hands, ripping it out from the damp earth above. The torn roots showered blood.

Tommy threw the knife to his cousin. "Got it!" shouted Mikey, snapping the blade out and cutting away at the flesh-eating root system. Blood squirted out like water through a tattered garden hose. Both men continued to fight with the killer roots, pulling at anything hanging.

The two men heard the sound of the backdoor creaking opening again.

"Quiet, I think he's coming," uttered Tommy. They heard the sound of shotguns above them.

"Over here!" whispered Mikey, pointing to a tunnel that was free of the tentacle roots. Tommy handed Mikey the flashlight as his cousin led the way. The two men crawled on their hands and knees about twenty feet before finding an opening.

Mikey dug his pointed shoes into the damp soil and climbed up, clearing away the final layer of grass and drooping pumpkin roots with the knife. He poked his head out from the hole. As he attempted to climb out, he was abruptly impaled by Mr. Rey's pitchfork, both tines plunging deep into his left shoulder. He cried out as blood poured from the wound. Quivering in pain, he slumped over, motionless.

"What the hell is going on up there?" asked Tommy, panic in his whisper. He tugged on his cousin's legs, but there was no response. The bloodied flashlight and knife dropped at his feet as Mr. Rey retracted his weapon and grabbed Mikey around the collar, pulling him up from the hole. He held Mikey at eye level and flashed a wicked smile. "You and your friend will make a lovely meal for my pumpkins."

Tommy picked up the knife and the flashlight then flashed the beam upward only to see streams of blood cascading downward. He slumped to the ground in horror, barely able to move a muscle. From above he heard his cousin groan – he was still alive. With a burst of energy, he wiped the blood off the flashlight and did an about face, crawling back over mud and bones towards the human compost pile. Frantic, he scrambled for the gasoline can, spreading a third of the contents around the killer vegetation amongst the dead bodies before climbing up, using a handful of the thickest roots as rope. He nudged his face out of the hole, peeking just above the pumpkin foliage. Mr. Rey was standing with his back to him.

"The hell you're feeding my cousin to your freak show pumpkins," growled Tommy under his breath. A few wandering creepers wrapped around Tommy's ankles, but he ripped them off with ease. He crawled over and hid behind a tree, eyeing the disturbing man. All Tommy was thinking about now was saving his cousin – and burning everything to the fucking ground . . . and below.

Mr. Rey began to drag Mikey's body towards the human compost pit. Tommy reached in his back pocket and searched for matches, but came up empty. "Shit," he muttered. Mikey had them.

Tommy crept on his knees, circling around the sea of red pumpkins, and hid behind a busted old tractor. He stood up and glanced over to the back porch where he spotted the shotgun. *Good, at least he didn't have his gun.* Tommy shifted over a few feet when he nearly stepped on a rusted shovel. He bent down and picked it up. It wasn't much, but he'd take it as a weapon.

Part of the shovel blade was broken away, but it had a nice point. *If these pumpkins are filled with blood, then they could have feelings,* Tommy thought, *I could draw Mr. Rey by jabbing at his revolting creations.*

Tommy eyed a large, fleshy red pumpkin, big as a beach ball, just in front of him. Still on his knees, Tommy harpooned the object. It made a high-pitched sound as blood gushed out like a broken water balloon. Mr. Rey turned, dropping Mikey's limp body to the ground. Tommy stood up and began jabbing at more pumpkins. There were more high-pitched cries, and more blood spilling onto the cold earth, the contrast in temperatures creating a reddish vapor.

"My pumpkins!" hollered Mr. Rey. "You're a dead man."

"Yeah, you said that before," countered Tommy. "But I'm still here. Guess that's why I'm known as Tommy Nine-Lives – and it aint' because I like cats. And before I kill you, you gotta tell what's up with your fucked-up pumpkins."

"Dinner," replied Mr. Rey rather stoically. He glanced up at the sky. "Sometimes friends like to pop in for takeout."

Tommy eyed a particularly large pumpkin, looking like it was ready to burst. He raised the shovel above his head. "Better tell 'em you're closed."

He brought the shovel down so hard the pumpkin exploded on impact. Mr. Rey stormed over, but the mobster was ready. As the tall man raised his pitchfork, Tommy launched the shovel like a harpoon, striking Mr. Rey right in the gut. He doubled over in pain, dropping the weapon at his feet. Tommy picked it up then ran to his cousin where he found a pack of matches tucked in Mikey's back pocket.

He scrambled back over to the hole, ready to drop a pair of lit matches when Mr. Rey stabbed Tommy just below his left shoulder blade with the sharp edge of the shovel, causing Tommy to recoil in pain. The burly man tumbled over, nearly falling into the human body pit. He rolled to his right, struggling to his feet as blood soaked his lower body.

As blood dropped to the ground, pumpkin vines propelled toward him like sharks sensing injured prey. Tommy reached for the pitchfork in the tall grass as Mr. Rey closed in. He grimaced in pain as he staggered out of harm's way. Regaining his bearings, Tommy began stalking Mr. Rey like a heavyweight fighter, keeping his opponent at bay by jabbing the pitchfork at him any time he approached. He peeked over Mr. Rey's shoulder, hoping to steer the crazed man towards the human compose pit.

"You're a fucking wacko, you know that?" yelled Tommy. "Think you can feed people to your zombie pumpkins?" Mr. Rey didn't reply as he backed away. Blood continued to drip from Tommy's gash. Mr. Rey was only a few feet away from the pit now.

Mr. Rey started uttering words under his breath. Tommy stood still, staring at the man. "I hate people who mumble; speak up, you fucking bastard!" screamed Tommy.

"I told you to get off of my property, didn't I?" said Mr. Rey, "But your yappy wife had to have one of my pumpkins. Now both you and your friend will be dead."

"Again with the threats," bested Tommy in full Casanova bravado.

A stream of vines ravenously curled around Tommy's bloodstained shoes. As he stepped forward, he stumbled, falling straight down on his face. The vine leaves fluttered up and down in a frontal assault. In no time, he was completely engulfed in pumpkin foliage.

"Now if you don't mind," said Mr. Rey, as he reached down and pried the pitchfork from Tommy's immobilized hand. Mr. Rey raised the garden tool high above his head; ready to plunge the tines straight into Tommy's chest. "Your wife will be next."

Tommy inner rage exploded. He mustered every ounce of violent energy in his frame and ripped through the entanglement of vines as if they were made of tissue paper. He flung the torn vegetation off his body just as Mr. Rey drove the tines deep into the ground. Tommy seized the knife from his back pocket, flicked the blade open, and lunged at Mr. Rey, stabbing him hard in the thigh. Mr. Rey toppled over on one knee, uttering an indecipherable cry. Before Mr. Rey could remove the weapon from his leg, Tommy stood up, gritted his teeth and launched a patented Mike Tyson-style left hook to the side of Mr. Rey's pallid face, shattering his left cheekbone.

Mr. Rey shook off the powerful blow and turned his head, now facing Tommy. He followed up with another full-force punch and backed away as the rest of Mr. Rey's face crumbled to the ground in pieces, like a shattered antique ceramic doll. "What the fuck?"

Inside, a harsh, narrow, darkened green facade emerged, eyes burning red in vitriol, upper and lower teeth piranha sharp. Two elongated incisors slowly emerged.

Not sure what he was witnessing, Tommy lunged again, throwing another thunderous left hook, this time Mr. Rey's midsection. Crack. Splintered fragments of white material fell to the ground. Tommy connected again with a right. This time, the rest of Mr. Rey's body fractured away, pieces falling on top of pieces. Mr. Rey's attire soon plummeted to the ground.

It hissed at Tommy.

"Oh shit."

"Happy Halloween, Tommy!" The words came out wobbly and mechanical. The thing outstretched its sinewy limbs, displaying lengthy sharpened fingers much like his pitchfork. Tommy jumped back as Mr. Rey jabbed his finger blades at Tommy. He darted over and clutched the pitchfork. He plunged the tines into the thing's narrow chest. It staggered backwards. Tommy held on to the pitchfork, steamrolling forward as he drove the thing into the pit. Tommy rushed over and quickly lit a handful of matches for good measure and tossed them in. Seconds later, flames soared skyward.

Tommy backtracked and headed over to his ailing cousin. He lifted him up and placed him at the back porch near the door for safety. He sought out the gasoline can, still half full, and marched around the pumpkin patch, dousing anything round and red. He dropped more matches, setting the back and side yard ablaze. As the pumpkins heated up, they began to explode, a sudden burst of red liquid showering the yard. Agonizing cries filled the whole back yard, scaring off the dozens of perched crows and scattered vultures. Tommy stumbled towards the barn to the right of the house and poured more gasoline around the wood structure.

He stepped inside and scanned the hay-filled floor before spotting numerous oak barrels, six total. Suspicious, Tommy removed one of lids. "Crapola." He proceeded to remove the rest.

Each barrel was filled with thousands of red pumpkin seeds. "Fucking A," he uttered. Tommy emptied the remaining contents of the gasoline canister around each barrel. He placed more hay around the barrels just in case then retrieved the matches from his pocket, lighting and dropping two into each barrel. As the flame grew intense, the seeds started exploding like popcorn. Next to the tractor, he dropped two more matches on the gas-soaked hay. In minutes, the old barn became engulfed in flames, smoke billowing out the gaping front entrance.

With the property almost fully immersed with flames, Tommy raced to the back of the house to retrieve his cousin's body. It wasn't there.

"Mikey!" He scoured the back yard, running over to the fiery human compost, but couldn't find him. "You shit monster!"

Tommy raced through the barbequed foliage and tried to open the back door. It was locked. He lifted up his stocky leg and busted the door wide open – now was no time to be quiet. Tommy man poked his head in. The darkened interior smelled just as bad as the pit. Tommy stumbled across the kitchen and found a mountain of filthy dishes almost toppling over in the dingy sink. Still holding the gasoline can, he poured some of the contents into an empty coffee can sitting on top of the mustard yellow countertop.

He searched out each and every room on the first floor but found nothing. The whole place was nearly void of furniture except for a ratty brown sofa chair, a small table with a lamp, and a Zenith color television that looked like it was left over from the Jimmy Carter years. Tommy hustled upstairs, but found the same thing: nothing. He poured gasoline on the hallway floor and ventured back downstairs. As he walked towards the kitchen to fill up the container again, he heard a groaning cry coming from the basement.

Tommy retrieved the pen flashlight from his back pocket and headed to the door. He crept down on each plank, barely making a sound. Reaching bottom, he followed a strange noise, almost like buzzing flies. Tommy heard his cousin moan again. He ambled over to a door sporting a foot-long crack. He pressed his ear against the grimy yellowed surface, paused, then bent down and peered through the slivered opening. Through a low wattage light bulb hanging from the ceiling, Tommy could see the thing about to bite into Mikey's bloodied neck as he lay motionless on a leaning wood table.

"Not a good idea, prune face!" snarled Tommy as he kicked in the door. The creature turned to attack, but Tommy hurled the gasoline straight into its eyes. He reached into his front pocket for the matches.

"Oh shit! Where are the freaking matches?" he screamed. The creature, screeching in agony, shook its head wildly from side to side. Tommy tried to get to his cousin, but the creature was too close. He frantically rummaged for anything to defend himself.

Behind him he found a broom . . . and more barrels filled with pumpkin seeds, thousands and thousands of them. The thing started to regain its composure.

"What are you gonna do, Tommy, brush me aside?" teased the formally Mr. Rey, now sneering, his emaciated frame charred like a briquette. Tommy's eyes darted between the creature and Mikey.

Tommy poked the broom at the thing like a lion tamer, hoping to keep it at bay. Mikey groaned, before slowly placing his fingers in his front pant pocket. He pulled out his custom-made gold lighter but struggled to flick it open. Tommy jabbed at the creature again, but it knocked the broom out of his hands.

"I told you to get off my property," the creature began saying repeatedly, quicker and faster then suddenly like a skipping record. "Get-get-get-get-get-get."

"Mikey, Hurry!"

Mikey reached back and flicked the lighter open – the flame shooting two inches high. Without looking, the injured man tossed it at the creature, setting it ablaze.

Quickly, the room became engulfed in flames. Tommy bent over to retrieve the lighter and picked Mikey up by the waist and carried him out from the burning room. He hurried over to the base of the stairs and placed Mikey's uninjured arm over his brawny shoulder. Struggling to reach the top, Tommy headed for the back door.

"The gas. Turn on the gas," gasped Mikey in a whisper, coughing.

"The what?"

"Turn on the . . ." Tommy shook his head, trying to understand his cousin. He retrieved what was left of the gas container and poured a trail along the living room and kitchen floor.

"Alright Mikey, let's get the hell out of here!"

Tommy barreled through the flames and smoke with Mikey and made it outside to safety. He took the gas container and finished up a trail of fuel ten feet outside the back door. He handed his cousin the lighter, and Mikey did the rest, igniting the trail of gasoline. The two started back to the car when the house exploded like a bomb, throwing both men to the ground. Tommy helped his cousin off the cold surface and the two headed down the embankment to the car. He aided Mikey into the rear seat, placing him on his back. Tommy slumped into the driver's seat, his body beaten and bloodied.

He adjusted the seat, tilting it back and then stared at the two structures, both engulfed in a sea of tangerine orange and chimney red.

Tommy rolled down the window and took a deep breath. He exhaled then reached for a pack of cigarettes hidden in a side compartment. He grumbled, unable to find a match. Mikey reached up and handed over the lighter, partially smeared in blood. He offered up a weak, but thankful smile. "Don't leave home without it," he whispered before resting his weary body on the black leather interior.

Tommy reached over and grasped his cousin's hand. "You did good, Mikey."

With his side throbbing in pain and clothes stained in blood, Tommy tried to digest what the hell had transpired this evening. He rubbed the bridge of his nose and tilted his head toward the towering flames, mesmerized. He dozed off.

Twenty minutes later, Tommy was startled by the sounds of blaring sirens. He crouched down as a pair of fire trucks came barreling down the deserted road heading towards Mr. Rey's property. Tommy repositioned the seat and started the car, headlights off, and drove off in the opposite direction to the nearest hospital.

Welcome to the Jungle

It was near closing time. Louis Breeden, branch manager at the secluded Mangrove Public Library, stared out at the ominous blackening sky from the panoramic window of the employee lounge. He glanced down at his watch and took a gulp of lukewarm coffee. Fifteen more minutes.

The brisk winds angled the driving rain, stirring rounded sea grape leaves like confetti. "Damn storm's gonna be a pain in the ass to drive home in," he muttered in his hardened voice. The quaint town of Mangrove, Florida was still feeling the residue from last week's tropical storm.

The first one hit the window full force, cracking it like a thrown rock. The next one hit even harder. Scores of them began pounding the ten-thousand square foot building from the air like falling bricks. Breeden jumped back in shocked amazement, dropping his prized orange Florida Gators mug to the floor. The screams of patrons inside the library echoed throughout the aging structure.

Breeden rushed to the door leading to the circulation desk. Two employees crouched under their desks in stunned disbelief. The motion sensor on the front glass doors froze, leaving the building wide open. Whatever was attacking the building was starting to find its way

65

inside. Breeden rushed over to the entrance, hurdling over a chair. He pressed the button to the automatic sliding glass doors but nothing happened. He then grabbed the doors with his bare hands and started pulling them together. Halfway in, the power kicked in and did the rest.

Almost instantaneously, blood splattered against the glass as a man begged to get back inside. Breeden tried to open it, but the door wouldn't budge. He could only stare in horror as they engulfed the man like ravenous sharks in a feeding frenzy, literally tearing the man apart at the seams.

"Everybody, take cover in the back, quickly, quickly," ordered Breeden. He picked up a dropped umbrella from the floor and opened it, doing his best to shield himself against the aerial assault.

"What the hell is going on?" cried Annie Croft, a 62-year old slender woman, who worked the reference desk. With her pencil-thin frame and uncontrolled frizzy hair, Croft had earned the endearing nickname 'Mop with a Masters' by homeless regulars. Her younger counterpart, Elaina Greer, was a part-time college student.

"I don't know," answered Breeden.

"They look like some sort of mutant bats," yelled Greer, who managed to swat away one strafing creature with a copy of Maurice Sendak's picture book, *Where the Wild Things Are*.

"Let's move – now!" shouted Breeden. A handful of people rushed into the back office. "First of all, is anyone hurt?"

"Tis but a scratch," Croft replied, who had suffered a minor wound on her right hand. Greer had a scrape on her forearm.

Maury Worthman, resident oddball and former postal worker, displayed scratches on both arms but appeared to be okay. The balding hippie in his late sixties sported a ponytail with vanilla white hair. He routinely explored government cover-ups and conspiracies.

Andrea Gonzales, a fourth-grade schoolteacher in her late thirties, and the boy appeared to be fine. Breeden advised the group to clean the wounds with soap and warm water ASAP.

Greer finished washing up then placed a band aide on the wound. "I wish I had my gun right about now."

"You and me both," said Breeden, a veteran hunter and weekend angler himself. Twenty years ago, he had briefly held the state record for catching the largest snook off the seashell capital of the world, Sanibel Island.

"You're Michael Wagner's younger brother, right?" Greer asked the schoolboy, trying to make him more at ease.

"Uh huh. I'm Chris."

Breeden, towering over the boy at six-foot-three inches, patted him on his shoulder. "Son, why don't you grab a seat and try to relax. Are you alone?"

"Um . . . yeah," Chris stammered. "But my mom is supposed to pick me up any minute." The boy, slight build with short blond hair, was doing his best to stay calm. He cleared his throat. "There were more people out there."

Breeden nodded, examining the cracks to the glass window. He tried the phones, but the lines were dead. "Folks, I don't know exactly what we're dealing with, but we need to secure this building – windows, doors, understood?" The group nodded.

"Stay here folks." He reached for a broom and tin dustpan in the closet before heading for the work area door. *Armed and dangerous*, he thought, feeling ridiculous. He opened the door a crack . . .

WHAM!

The assault started up again, sounding like thumping kettledrums as the objects pelted the building. The survivors in the back office shifted towards the panoramic window, mesmerized by the flying creatures.

"There must be hundreds of them," said Chris in astonishment, turning to the adults. As he turned back, a creature splattered against the glass, sending the boy to the floor in startled fright.

"Maybe we all better move away from the window," said Croft as she helped him up.

The black winged creatures were two feet in length. Their rough, textured bodies and extended talons appeared lizard-like, a throwback to prehistoric times. Their mouths resembled barracudas, lined with oversized dagger teeth. The eyes were neon yellow with dark green slits for pupils, their wiry tails whipping through the air like stingrays.

And they kept on coming.

Breeden peered through the crack of the employee doorway. Through the darkened building he could hear the frenzied barrage of the creatures. He stepped out and slid past the circulation desk before posting up behind a round column. Breeden poked his head, surveying the scene. The emergency lights provided just enough light for him to decipher the heavily blood-soaked carpeting. He stepped just beyond the reference bookcases when he found two adult patrons, mauled to death. He knelt down to see if he knew who they were. He didn't recognize what was left of their faces; vacationers most probably.

As Breeden stood up, a creature shot out like a clay skeet, striking him in the right shoulder. He managed to partially block it with the dustpan, but it left a gash near his collarbone.

"Holy Christ!" He fended off the creature, swatting it with the broom. Breeden swung at the stunned animal and sent it flying into the front glass door. With his adrenalin flowing like river rapids, he stormed over, raised his right foot and brought down his size twelve Timberland boot on the creature's neck, killing it instantly. "Little shit."

Breathing heavily, he double-checked the front door then surveyed the rest of the building. He found another dead person before stumbling upon two more bodies.

Breeden heard a strange chirping sound above him and froze.

There, three creatures were clinging to the square ceiling tiles with their elongated talons.

"Oh sugar," uttered Breeden. He made a mad dash for the back door. The three creatures darted after him. He picked up the umbrella left on the circulation desk and tried to fend them off. "A little help here!"

"Damn you!" cursed Breeden, desperately trying to open the back door as one of the creatures snapped at his hands. The door burst open as Greer unleashed a double-barrel of buckshot, killing two of the creatures.

Greer fired once more, obliterating the remaining creature as it flew towards her, before darting back inside. "Piss heads." She locked the door and headed to the kitchen to wash the blood off her hands and face.

"Where the hell did you get the gun?" asked Breeden, grimacing in pain, his hands littered with bite marks.

"My truck," answered Greer. "I'm not gonna take crap from these flying shits. Besides, my dad's a former marine. You think I grew up playing with Barbie dolls?"

"Thank God they didn't attack you out there in the parking lot," replied Breeden. How'd you manage that?"

"Quiet as a mouse, and ran like hell, boss."

Breeden smiled then went into the kitchen and washed up. He snagged the package of gauze bandages from the first aid kit and mummified both bleeding hands. Thirsty, he reached into the olive green refrigerator and popped open a ginger ale, guzzling it before slumping down in a chair. "These pesky little buggers are—"

"Aliens," blurted out Maury Worthman.

"Don't be ridiculous," said Croft. "It's probably some sort of . . ."

"Sort of what?" prodded Worthman. "Some experiment gone wrong?

"If you ask me, there's something very weird going on in the 'Glades," said Greer. "Think of all that pesticide runoff and irresponsible people dumping exotic animals. It's like they've created some sort of . . . mutant paella recipe."

"Yeah, like that sounds more plausible," chimed Croft.

"Or maybe the storm brung 'em," added Worthman. "Hell, it's South Florida!"

"Folks, whatever it is, we need to find help or we're in deep trouble," said Gonzales.

"Well, the electricity's been spotty at best," said Breeden, "and the phones are dead."

"And as we've come accustom to out here in the middle of the freaking Amazon: the cell phone reception completely blows," added Greer.

"Thank you for putting it so eloquently," jabbed Croft.

"I'm telling you, it's aliens!" begged Worthman. The adults were arguing with each other and offering up their theories when the boy spoke up.

"Stop it!" Please, just . . . stop," chided Chris. Everyone quieted down. "My mom could be out there and I don't want her attacked by these flying freaks. I need to know if she's okay."

Breeden looked over at the boy. "You're right, kid. We'll go look for her."

"What kind of car does she drive?" asked Greer.

"It's a red Subaru wagon," said Chris. "She should have been here by now."

"We'll find her," said Breeden, reassuring the boy.

Breeden gathered up two pairs of scissors and wrapped layers of gray duct tape to attach them to the end of the broom.

"What, no dustpan this time?" smiled Greer. "If that doesn't work, I got you covered," she added, brandishing her shotgun.

"Appreciate it," said Breeden as he finished up. "I feel like we're in one of those Godawful SyFy Channel movies."

The two slipped out the side employee entrance. It was dark out, not a sound except for croaking frogs and ringing crickets. The library was surrounded by white and black mangrove trees, along with towering sea grapes. The night air felt humid and heavy, typical for September in southwest Florida.

"I don't see any of them; that's a good thing," whispered Greer.

"That's what I'm worried about," replied Breeden. "I think they're hiding, ready to attack us. We need to be quiet, not a sound." Just then, he stepped on a fallen branch, snapping it in two.

"So much for being quiet," whispered Greer.

The two half-circled the building. The two spotted the red Subaru, one of the headlights broken, the windshield a mesh of shattered glass. "Damn, that's got to be her car," said Breeden.

"Oh, shit," answered Greer.

They crouched down and scurried up to the battered passenger side door. A woman was slumped over on the steering wheel. "Oh God, no," sighed Greer, cupping her hands over her mouth. There was a groan.

"Holy crap, she's alive," said Greer as Breeden peered through the other side. He tapped on the glass and called to her. The woman slowly lifted her head, still in a daze. She was able to unlock the driver's side door. The door screeched as Breeden opened it.

"Ma'am, are you okay?" asked Breeden.

The woman suddenly cried out. "My son! Where's my son?"

Breeden could tell the woman was in stunned disbelief. There was blood on the left side of her head and a cut just above her right eye.

"Ma'am, Chris is safe inside the library."

Greer, standing next to him perked up. "You hear that?"

"Hear what?" replied Breeden. "I don't . . ."

"Get inside the car!" yelled Greer.

Breeden shifted around and got into the front passenger seat as Greer got in the back and shut the door, locking it.

"You hear anything?" she asked.

"Nothing," said Breeden. Through the windshield he suddenly eyed a hovering black mass just above a trio of sabal palms. "Oh shit, here they come!"

In seconds, the bombardment commenced, pounding the all-wheel drive vehicle into submission. Breeden shielded the young boy's mother as Greer reached over to lock the back doors.

A large creature hit the back window, cracking it. Another slammed into the rear driver's side window next to Greer, penetrating through. Taking off her black jean jacket and covering her hands for protection, she grabbed the thrashing creature by the neck and slammed it down on a pointed shard of glass. The creature gushed a deep crimson all over the back seat.

"Let's switch seats, ma'am," said Breeden in a firm voice, sliding behind Chris's mom. He pushed the seat back and started the car. "Hold on, folks!"

Breeden looped around to the back of the library and headed for the employee entrance. More creatures engulfed the windshield, blocking his vision. He placed the wipers on high, clearing the view momentarily, but then . . . SLAM.

The wagon crashed against the sturdy bike rack, setting off the airbags. "Christ almighty!" said Breeden. "I'm gonna get us all killed. You two okay?"

The injured mother nodded; she was a bit shaken but otherwise fine. Greer was the same. Breeden laid on the horn. Moments later, Croft opened the door a crack and noticed the dented hood of the car. She scanned the night sky and waved frantically.

"Hurry, hurry!"

"On three," said Breeden. "One, two, three." They rushed from the vehicle and spilled into the safe confines of the musty library.

"Mom, mom," cried Chris, hugging her like he hadn't seen her in a year. The boy helped her into a chair. Breeden hurried over to the kitchen to retrieve some ice and paper towels. "Are you okay?" The boy grimaced at the sight of the wounds on his mother. He'd never seen his mom hurt in any way, ever.

"I'm fine son, I'm fine, thank you." She hugged him, collecting her thoughts before turning to Breeden. "What are those things?"

Croft turned to Worthman, shushing him before he could spout any of his kooky theories, although his ideas were growing on her. The hippie shook his head, flustered.

"Our best guess is those flying freaks came from the Glades," said Greer.

"Or aliens," added Worthman who couldn't help himself, eying Croft.

"That actually sound more plausible," said Chris's mother. Worthman gloated. Croft seethed.

"Alien or no alien, we gotta get a hold of someone to help us," said Breeden.

Another wave of creatures pounded against the panoramic window, etching out more and more cracks like lines on a map.

"Damn it," said Breeden. "Another barrage like that and the window's gonna go." He reached for the duct tape and zigzagged strips all over the larger fissures.

Greer tried her cell again. "Hold on everybody, I got a signal!" The phone rang . . . and rang. "Come on, come on, pick up, Dad."

The electricity flickered on. "Finally," smiled Breeden. His face suddenly turned to marble as he heard a motorized sound. "Oh no." He stumbled over to the door leading to the circulation desk. He turned to everyone. "We've got trouble."

The boy ran over, followed by Greer. The two poked their heads out. "What is it?" asked Croft.

"The front doors are open again," noted Breeden. "All of you better get inside my office and lock the door just in case that back window breaks."

"I've got two shells left," said Greer. "I'm staying with you."

"Ok, but we gotta make this quick. The rest of you, go to my office now!" The survivors scurried into Breeden's office as he and Greer rumbled their way towards the front door of the building. The lights inside the library dimmed.

Greer, seeing nothing but a wide-open invitation into the darkness, stood ready. Breeden pressed the button repeatedly to close the doors, but they remained frozen. He placed the broom down and stood between the open doorway, reaching out to pull them together like before. There was a screeching metal sound.

Breeden paused for a moment – and only for a moment when the creatures swooped down and attacked him. He yelled in agony, falling to the ground. Breeden tried to reach for the broom but was overwhelmed by the sudden onslaught. Greer pointed her gun, poised to shoot, but didn't want to risk injuring Breeden. She cried out, seeing Breeden's hand desperately trying to reach out to her. She used the butt of the shotgun and began teeing off on the creatures left and right.

Seeing her boss momentarily free and clear, Greer fired twice into the swarm of frenzied creatures. "Eat that, you fucking bastards!"

Worthman ran over to help Greer drag Breeden back inside. Breeden was a bloodied mess but still conscious. They carried him to the back office. Worthman placed him on the floor and propped his head up with a jacket hanging on the back of his chair.

"Oh my God, are you okay," asked Greer in tears.

"And I thought palmetto bugs were a nuisance," jested Breeden, coughing. His breathing was slight. Croft went to the kitchen and retrieved a large amount of paper towels, wetting them with cool water. She knelt down and cleaned up the numerous wounds.

The creatures started bombarding the back window again, the cracks spreading. One more direct shot and they'd all be dead.

"What's that?" asked the boy.

"You hear it too?" cried Croft.

Croft, Greer, and Worthman stayed by Breeden's side as Gonzales and the boy hurried to gaze out the window.

A helicopter buzzed the library, circling again and again. "What's it doing?" asked Gonzales,

The helicopter unloaded a heavy florescent mist that lit up the night sky like sparklers.

"It's glowing," beamed Chris.

Suddenly they heard a thud . . . then another. The creatures started falling, pelting the library building and the surrounding parking lot.

"Wait," said Greer. She hurried over to a side window near the supply room. "It must be some sort of poison!"

"A what?" squawked Croft. "Did you just say poison?"

Greer perked up. "Whoever's up there is spraying those little SOBs like they're mosquitoes."

"And?" asked Gonzales.

"They're dropping like flies," cried Chris in delight.

"But who's doing it?" inquired Worthman. "The CIA? FBI? MIB?"

Greer's phone rang. "Hello? Dad? I'm so glad you were able to get a hold . . . What? I'm fine, I'm fine. Uh, okay. I promise." Her dad's voice was partially downed out from the sound of the whirling chopper. "I PROMISE!"

"What did your dad have to say?" asked Croft. The rest of the survivors gathered around the young woman like huddling football players. She cleared her throat, feeling totally bewildered.

"My dad . . ."

"What? What?" begged Worthman.

"Um, he strongly insisted we all stay in here for a while until they're finished, preferably in a sealed office or bathroom. That roll of duct tape might be come in handy."

"That's it?" asked Croft.

"Finished with what?" asked Chris.

"The extermination process." Greer turned to Croft. "Oh, and we better keep this all quiet . . . or else."

"Or else?" replied Croft. "Oh, I don't like the sound of that."

Greer took a deep breath and exhaled, eyeing Worthman. "Maybe we should listen to what the hippie has to say more often."

Worthman grinned.

Croft seethed.

The Shack

Trevor Donnelly, a sophomore at Miami University in Ohio, returned home from college for the Thanksgiving break. His parents picked him up from Newark Airport early Wednesday afternoon. Trevor stared aimlessly outside as they drove home. Unfortunately, he recognized the familiar landscape of Kennett, New Jersey and knew exactly where he was.

His stomach churned as they drove down Wickham Road, past the house where his friends were brutally killed in 1982, the year he graduated high school. He always steered clear of Wickham Road, but his dad had forgotten.

"I'm sorry, I should have taken . . ." Dad glanced in the rearview mirror at his son, who was sitting in the back seat and leaning his head against the window.

"It's okay." Trevor turned up the volume on his Walkman, trying to drown out any invasive thoughts. The gangly guitar sounds of "A Forest" by the Cure leaked from the cheap headphones. His mom turned. "We're almost home, dear."

They pulled into the driveway, greeted by his two older brothers, who were throwing the football in the front yard, and their three-year-old adopted Siberian husky Trevor renamed MacReady, after the lead character from John Carpenter's 1982 movie *The Thing*. He offered a quick hello to his brothers as he grabbed his duffle bag full of dirty clothes from the trunk and headed inside.

"How's he doing?" asked the eldest brother, Will, flipping the football in his right hand.

"This isn't a good time of year for him," replied Dad.

The other brother, Brian, two years younger than Will at age twenty-four, chimed in as they walked into the house. "There's nothing he could have done."

Everyone clammed up as Trevor reappeared from the laundry room. Mom had already fixed son number three a stacked baloney and cheese sandwich on whole wheat with chips and a glass of sweetened iced tea.

"It's okay, guys, you can talk; I'm not gonna melt." Trevor was mentally worn down from a sea of marathon study sessions. Exam time was a complete ball buster and he just wanted to crash.

Trevor gobbled up his late afternoon lunch, let out a hefty belch – forgetting he wasn't at school anymore, and trudged upstairs to unwind. Mom frowned. She had always emphasized excellent manners for her three boys.

"I hope we're not spending all that money so you can be a layabout!"

"And don't forgot living expenses," groaned Dad.

"Excuse me!" bellowed Trevor.

"Better," said Mom. "Let us know if you need anything."

Trevor closed his bedroom door, pulled the deep blue curtains together, and plopped down on the full-sized mattress. The one at MU was wafer thin and about as comfortable as a sheet of plywood. He quickly fell fast asleep. It didn't take long for the nightmare to return.

***

It was 1982, Thanksgiving evening. Like most late Novembers in New Jersey, it was cold, raw, and damp, with an outside chance of snow. Rather than joining his preppy senior class friends at the cookie cutter bar/restaurant in town, he opted – like most of the time, to hang out at the shack with his other friends, the ones that preferred wearing concert t-shirts and torn Levis – never a Polo brand or Lacoste garment in sight.

The shack was a decrepit twelve-by-twelve unpainted wood structure – more like a pitched-roof barn with open doorways at both ends. It was nestled on a hill a couple of hundred feet behind his best friend Rick Weber's house. No one knew who built it, but it was a cool place to drink beers, listen to music, and complain how much it sucked to live in a no-fun suburban town.

Trevor was the only senior of the group. At eighteen years old, he was still waiting for any form of facial growth to sprout. Although he looked younger than his friends, who were all juniors in high school, he could purchase beer legally. He routinely gathered up the beer funds from his friends before hitting the local liquor store. The employee behind the counter used to scrutinize his driver's license like a gemologist examining a finely cut diamond. The bearded man, late forties, was never one hundred percent convinced Trevor was of legal drinking age, but it said so on his license.

Partying Thanksgiving night was quickly becoming a ritual. After dining on everything turkey and watching football all day, it was time to get away from the family and relatives. It was just past eight in the evening when Trevor arrived at Rick's rundown ranch style house. The gravel driveway lasted forever with pine trees lined up like coarse green statues on each side. The real selling point of the property was the eight-plus acres of secluded forest, the majority set in the back yard, heading uphill. The next closest home was a quarter mile in every direction.

As custom, Trevor pulled up near the garage entrance and beeped the chirpy, high-pitched horn on his 1974 orange Saab 99, appropriately nicknamed the pumpkin mobile. Trevor was a walking monster movie encyclopedia and loved Halloween, so anything orange was of no surprise. His favorite football team even donned orange and black.

Rick strolled outside, zipping up his jacket and got in. His mom had just left for the weekend to visit a family member in nearby Pennsylvania. Rick was an only child, living with his mom, now divorced. As long as her son got good grades and stayed out of trouble, she didn't care what he did. The latter tended to be the issue. Trevor, on the other hand, had to live up to the expectations of his two older brothers, both who graduated from top universities and excelled in athletics.

Trevor was slender, a bit goofy, quick witted, and a creative writer, but solidly average at sports, although he did manage to win a medal in summer camp for woodcarving and archery. His parents realized pestering their youngest son constantly wasn't going to work. Trevor was a thoroughly entrenched B-type personality, studying little yet still managing respectable grades. If he heard his parents utter, 'If you only applied yourself a little more' one more time he was going to hitchhike to Nova Scotia.

Rick pulled out a cigarette and was about to light it. "You should know better," said Trevor, who had a strict rule of no smoking – of any kind, in his car. He hated it.

"Come on man," replied Rick, "We're best friends."

"No can do; you know how I despise cigarettes." Trevor's dad was a former smoker, finally quitting after being diagnosed with throat cancer years earlier. Getting cancer was a sure-fire way of making anyone give up smoking.

Rick shook his head. "Sometimes I can't figure you out."

"Join the club," replied Trevor who slid a cassette of the Who's *Quadrophenia* into the recently installed car stereo – side two; song number one: 5:15. "Out of my brain on a train!" he crooned.

Trevor backed up before veering off the driveway. He headed up the rocky trail, just wide enough for his tangerine car.

Ever since his junior year in high school when he and his friends discovered beer, Trevor and Rick, along with their cohorts Joe Coslett and twins Peter and Thomas Lewis, savored many a weekend evening building fires in the designated pit, listening to music and, of course, consuming adult beverages.

The Lewis brothers, both tall and lanky with curly dark brown hair, shared the same laidback demeanor. Both were aspiring guitar players, and quite good. Joe played bass, thumping out bombastic riffs. The guy could polish off a twelve-pack and still remain sober. No wonder he started shrooming to reach a better buzz.

The twins, along with Joe and Rick, had started a band three years prior and had progressed respectively, although having a band named *The Screw Ups* didn't exactly conjure up long-term success. Thinking up band names when you're stoned is never a good idea.

The brothers were already up at the shack, dropped off by their older brother. They were sprucing up the circular grounds, rearranging bowling ball-sized stones around the fire pit. They usually rummaged through the forest looking for wood for the fire, but this time Joe pulled up in his fire red engine Chevy pickup truck filled with split logs. Joe stood six feet-one and sported frizzy blond, surfer-type approved hair and was a sure-fire class clown. There was a story where he once answered every question on a middle school science test with the word 'trout', and somehow managed to get one correct.

"We're gonna have a real fire for a change," said Joe, a cigarette dangling from the corner of his mouth.

"Nice bro," said Peter. "Where'd you get?"

"The forest, nipple head," replied Joe. "Duh." The four dug out their wallets and handed over whatever cash they could muster to cover the cost. "I was getting tired of looking for wood like Daniel fucking Boone."

The temperature hovered around the low-forties: not exactly the ideal drinking weather, but that's what bonfires were for. Despite the recent downpours, pockets of snow still remained from last weeks' surprise blanketing. Trevor and Rick took a case of Budweiser and an extra six-pack out from the pumpkin mobile and placed the bottles in the patches of snow.

"At least we don't have to worry about warm beer," said Thomas, who brought along two cans of Pringles chips and a bag of Bugles. Occasionally they'd roast hot dogs, although everyone was still plump full of Thanksgiving eats. The twins always thought it was gross how Trevor doused his hotdog with ketchup instead of mustard.

"Hey, what's with the Mexican beer?" inquired Joe. He and the rest of the guys swilled on nothing but the King of Beers, Budweiser.

"When we went on vacation to Mexico last summer, my dad let me try a Corona and it was tasty. I think he got a bit concerned how much I liked it. There were people at the hotel pool who actually put a slice of lime in it."

Trevor reached into his jacket pocket and pulled out a small Ziploc bag of cut limes, showing it off. He took one out and tried shoving it down the narrow, clear neck. "Damn, I cut it too thick. *Puta!*"

"*Puta*? What's *puta* mean?" asked Rick.

"I think it means 'whore' in Spanish," answered Trevor, finally jamming the slice of bitter fruit inside the bottle. He took a sip, not fully embracing the tartness of the lime, cringing a bit. "Uh, *muy bien*!"

"Lime in beer," shrugged Joe. "*Que stupido*!" He proceeded to guzzle down a cold Bud in one big gulp. The rest of the guys applauded in unison.

"Who's got the paper?" asked Trevor, itching to start the fire.

"Rolling papers," blurted out Joe in laughter, as he sparked up a joint. Everyone looked at each other, figuring someone was supposed to be the go-to newspaper boy. No one was particularly eager to make the long trek back down the slick, muddy hill to Rick's house for supplies.

"Time to put my Cub Scout skills to work," said Trevor. He tore up the cardboard from the case of beer and tucked it strategically between the logs. In no time, the five were feeling warm, cracking open beers and getting toasted.

"Mr. College Boy – always the thinker," said Rick, who blew off the SAT test last month to go camping instead with the Lewis twins. As a junior, he had to get his ass in gear or it'd be community college for sure, and in an upper middle class town like theirs, attending anything with the word 'community' in it was strictly taboo.

"You're going too, dick weed," replied Trevor, who knew his best friend would like nothing more than live outside the Garden State for nine months out of the calendar year. The two had even discussed attending the same university.

"How about you," asked Trevor, addressing the twins. "You guys thinking of college?"

"Hell no," boasted Peter. "I'm gonna be a rock star!" He stood up and mimicked The Who's Pete Townsend, windmilling with the stripped four-foot tree branch Trevor was whittling. "We don't get fooled again!"

His brother Thomas rolled his eyes. "You're doing the windmill backwards, numb nuts."

"Since when did you give a damn about college?" asked Peter. "I didn't think it was possible, but you're lazier than us."

"Ha, ha," replied Trevor, grabbing the branch away from Peter. "Everybody in my family graduated from college, so you know I gotta go too. Hell, I hear it every freaking day about the importance of an education; my mom's a teacher, remember?" He took a hefty gulp of beer and belched. "God, if my mom heard that, I'd be grounded for a week. Sometimes I wish I had your parents."

"No you don't, bro," snapped Thomas. "They might bug you and all, but at least they care. Ours could give a shit. As long as we're out of view, not spoiling one of their precious dinner parties, everything's cool."

Trevor was taken aback. Usually the conversation was light and fun. Tonight's was awkward and more truthful – not one cartoon character impersonation to be found.

Joe had already polished off four beers before anyone had reached two. "I say do what the hell you want to do."

"That was quite profound," replied Trevor.

"Thanks man – what's 'profound' mean?"

Trevor was about to answer his friend when he heard a distant howl echoing high up the hill. Four of the five paid no attention to it, but Trevor perked up, looking deep into the blackened woods. His horror movie imagination quickly kicked into gear.

"Did anyone hear that?" The crackling sound of the imposing fire seemed to obscure the noise. No one paid attention.

Two hours later, with the alcohol settling in, Trevor and Joe did their dead-on Black Knight vs. King Arthur scene from *Monty Python and the Holy*

Grail. Joe always did a great job hobbling around on one leg.

"We'll call it a draw," said Trevor, as he placed the whittled branch in between his leather belt.

There was another howl, this one sounding deeper and closer than the previous one. All five turned towards the hill. They heard occasional stray dogs before; maybe this one was a newcomer to the scene.

Joe stood up, staggering a little. He was halfway through his second six-pack. "Time to use the little boy's tree," he said in a slurred English accent. Rick went over to the woodpile and grabbed a couple more logs.

Joe stumbled up the hill behind the shack and out of view. "Hey, I'm a new superhero – The Urinator! So you better not piss me off!" A chorus of boos rang out.

Rick got up to get another beer. "Who's thirsty?"

Peter and Thomas raised their hands like they were back in kindergarten. Trevor kept his personal stash close by. He took out his favorite bottle opener, shaped like a shark, and popped open his beer as Rick handed bottles to the twins.

Halfway through his, Peter called out. "What, is Joe setting a pissing record?"

"It'll be a flood coming down any minute," said Rick.

"Guy drinks like a freaking fish," said Thomas.

"How do you know how much fish drink?" chided Peter.

"I don't know – they live in water so they must drink a lot, like every day," replied Thomas. "How the hell do I know – they're fish!"

"Guys," said Trevor. "Maybe he passed out."

"After nine beers? No way," said Thomas. "Fourteen, maybe."

"Should someone check on him?" asked Rick.

"I'm not his goddamned babysitter," said Peter, stuffing his face with potato chips. He flipped one Pringle on top of another and placed them in his mouth like a duck before consuming both.

"Oh, for Christ's sake," barked Thomas. "Hey Joe, everything all right up there?" No answer.

Thomas shrugged at his brother and nodded. The two got up and cut through the shack then followed the path uphill. Trevor watched as the two bickered back and forth.

"Glad I don't have any siblings," said Rick. "You get along with your brothers, right?"

"Sometimes," answered Trevor, "But most of the time I feel like the black sheep of the family." He poured a few Pringles into his hand when he suddenly turned towards the woods.

"What was that?" Trevor called out, now standing up, his voice filled with apprehension. "Shouldn't they be back by now?"

"You know what I think?" declared Rick, raising his voice. "I think they're all playing a damn practical joke on us – you know how idiotic they can get. They're like freaking Thing One and Thing two, only on acid." Trevor almost snorted beer from his nose.

Both were about to sit back down and continued drinking when they heard a thunderous snarl. The reverberating sound filled both teens with goose bumps.

"That was way too close," uttered Trevor, as he reached for the branch, now pointed.

"Maybe it's a rabid dog," suggested Rick.

Trevor stood up, peering deep into the dark forest. "That doesn't sound like a dog to me,"

"Oh shit, I think I see something!" cried Rick, panic in his voice. He got up, tripping over a log, then unexpectedly bolted down the hill to his house.

"Where the hell are you going?" yelled Trevor, who stood there dumbfounded. A sea of trepidation filled his gut. Something wasn't right. Trevor turned his head back towards the shack, hearing something large galloping downhill. He backtracked over to his car, about to get in when he heard a scream. It was Rick.

He heard his friend cry for help. He froze, but there was only silence. Seconds later, he could make out something. It sounded like his dog MacCready when he's chewing relentlessly on one of those meaty butcher bones. But this sounded more savage, more guttural. Trevor dashed over to his car and pulled out his keys. He meekly called out to his friend but felt like he already the outcome.

"Rick? You okay?

He heard the sounds of snapping tree limbs coming up the hill. Oh shit."

Trevor quietly opened the door to his car and got in. He closed it then crouched down as low as he could. He was hyperventilating, terrified. Did his best friend just get killed by an animal? A crazed maniac, maybe? And what about his other friends? Were they all dead too? What the hell was happening?

He heard a reverberating growl, followed by heavy footsteps. Something stalked right by his car. Trevor's eyes darted to the door, realizing he hadn't lock it. He raised his quivering hand, about to press the lock down when a stream of hot breath fogged up the driver's side window. Trevor peered up, barely making out the image.

Burning red, hypnotic eyes stared back at him. Trevor's almost popped out of their sockets. He couldn't blink. His mouth went Sahara dry.

A towering creature started to scratch and claw at the door, jiggling the door handle. Trevor sprang up in the seat and locked it just in time, accidently turning on the cassette player. Music boomed though the oval shaped 6x9 Pioneer speakers.

The creature roared before driving its claws directly into the roof. Trevor panicked as he fumbled for the keys wedged deep in his jean pocket. His hands were trembling as he stuck the key into the ignition located between the bucket seats. He started the car then laid on the tinny horn. The creature retracted its claws and pushed against the car. Trevor sat up and put the car in reverse, but he backed up too fast and smacked into a large rock.

"Oh shit." Trevor righted himself. The creature stared directly at him.

It was tall and muscular yet sinewy, covered in matted dark brown fur. The steak knife claws dangled like shards of glass. It snarled, baring its long, ragged teeth that were stained with blood. Trevor thought of his friends, all presumably and brutally killed. Only he was left.

The crouching beast lunged forward just as Trevor gunned the four-cylinder automatic. The car knocked the creature square in the gut, sending it directly into a soaring pine tree. The creature doubled over in pain, now struggling to get up.

"R. J. MacReady wouldn't take things lying down and neither will I," yelled Trevor. "For my friends, you son of a bitch."

Trevor wheeled a tight K-turn between the rocks and trees before positioning the car directly in front of the roaring fire ten yards away. Ramming that fucker into the fire and barbequing his werewolf ass sounded like a good menu option. He looked back, but the creature was gone.

"Damn it! Where are you, you prick!"

Trevor craned his neck, peering out in every direction. He wanted to kill this nightmare right here and now. He waited impatiently for what seemed like hours, jumping at every sound. A half hour ticked by. Trevor tried to take in deep breaths. One thing he knew was hyperventilating was a bad thing. Stay calm and let's kill this motherfucker.

He looked over at both door locks, double-checking them for the umpteenth time. The car rumbled, but he noticed the gas gage was nearing empty.

It started snowing. Trevor placed the wipers on intermittent. He dozed off for a brief moment then sat up straight. He adjusted the rear-view mirror – and screamed.

The creature was there, glaring through the back window. Those eyes, like burning embers, bore right through him. It leaped onto the hood of the car. Trevor instinctively floored the gas, stopping short of the fire. The wolf creature skidded off the slick metal and onto the snow-covered ground.

Trevor quickly backed up and floored it again, striking the beast right into its muscular chest. The thing went flying, a bull's-eye directly into the fire. The flames were still high, sufficient enough to scorch the creature. The wolf wailed as it emerged from the pit, its body partially seared. Trevor backed up again then zeroed directly at the creature, propelling it back into the firepit again. This time, Trevor shot forward, pinning the werewolf underneath a ton of steel and rubber.

"Yeah," screamed Trevor, triumphantly.

He paused for a moment then thought. "Oh shit!" He panicked, thrusting the door open before running for safety. The creature thrashed its limbs and struggled under the weight of the car now engulfed in flames. Seconds later, the car exploded, throwing Trevor back against the stacked logs, knocking him out cold.

An hour later, Trevor awoke, shivering and covered with a light dusting of snow. He stood up, his head throbbing in pain. He shook his head, removing the cobwebs from the blow he had suffered. He picked up the branch he was whittling and used it to help himself up.

It was dead quiet. He saw the can of Pringles and empty beer bottled littered around the firepit, now filled with glowing embers, along with one smoldering orange

Saab 99. All at once, the horrific events of the evening flooded Trevor's memory. He eyed the shack and headed that way. He struggled up the incline past the wooden structure and called out to his friends. The smell of burnt rubber was making him nauseous. He knelt down and barfed behind a large rock. While kneeling, he glanced to his right and saw blood. And lots of it. *Oh God.*

Trevor firmly clutched the pointed stick with both hands as he ambled up the hill. He discovered a mangled deer but nothing else. He heard footsteps. His eyes got big as he surveyed the dark woods. He picked up his pace and lumbered past to the firepit, down towards his friend's house when he heard a cough.

"Rick?" Trevor called out. "Is that you?" He heard it again.

Trevor followed the noise. It was coming from the firepit. He spotted a body near the front of his car. He jumped back realizing it was the werewolf. Trevor was hit by a sudden rush of adrenalin. He raised the stick high, ready to plunge it deep into the heart of the beast. He shifted over for a better angle.

"For my friends, you hairy piece of shit."

"Trevor?" whispered a voice.

"Oh my God, Rick?"

Trevor knelt down and brushed away small pieces of debris from the body. "How, what . . ." Tears welled up. He couldn't believe it. Trevor grasped Rick's hand and squeezed it. He moved closer trying to make out what his friend was struggling to say.

"Hairy piece of shit?" uttered Rick, with a frail smile.

Tears rolled down Trevor's face. "I am so sorry, Rick." He bent down closer as his best friend spoke again.

"Mmmooore."

"What was that?" Trevor positioned his ear centimeters away from Rick's bloodied mouth, who repeated the line. Rick's head then slumped over. There was a howl.

Trevor stood up and peered deep uphill into the charred forest. "Oh shit."

A sea of red eyes lit up the forest as more wolves cried out. Seconds later, He could feel the stampeding creatures fast approaching.

Trevor raced down the gravel driveway and hit the pavement running for his life, not looking back.

****

Trevor awoke from his nap, groggy and hungry. He opened his bedroom door and called out downstairs. There was no answer. Trevor was hoping his family went out to pick up pizza. One thing he really missed while away at college was good Jersey pizza. The sauce had that distinctively sweet flavor. He felt rested, in a much better frame of mind than before. He glanced at his clock.

"Midnight? Christ, I've been asleep for almost ten hours?" Trevor stretched out his arms and sighed.

He called out again, this time much louder. "Mom, Dad?"

His room was stuffy. He went over to the bedroom window and opened it. He took in a deep breath. The brisk air felt good, like a splash of cold water on the face.

Suddenly, chills sprinted through Trevor's body as he heard the familiar deep, resonating howls.

And they were close.

Night of the Clippies

Chapter 1

The late October night sky was clear and full of stars, with a gentle push of wind coming from the east. Margaret Braeburn, thoroughly entrenched in her sixties and sporting all the vivacious curves of a middle linebacker, strode outside carrying a wicker laundry basket full of bedsheets. According to Margie, a nickname used only by her closest friends, the night air always seemed to make them smell fresher.

Her husband Ralph had died fifteen years ago, but she barely missed a beat with the chores and tribulations of owning a thirty-acre farm, one she'd worked on every day for the last forty years. She was the type of person who'd trim her toenails with a pair of garden shears, was rough as a pair of work boots, blunt force honest, yet always generous.

The goats were always the last to get cozy at bedtime. Everything else on four legs or webbed feet had succumbed to a hard day of doing nothing in particular, all asleep in and around the faded red barn. Margaret took in a deep breath, savoring the upper

New York state air of St. Lawrence County: crisp and clean. She was a country gal through and through.

The night sky suddenly exploded into a meteor shower, a burst of tiny flaming lights. *Shooting stars maybe?* Margaret seemed unfazed. She had barely been impressed by that "borealis thing" as she had referred to it when she'd spotted natures' lightshow on a family trip to Alaska a bunch of years ago

Margaret draped the white nylon clothesline with queen-size bedroom sheets first, colored in subtle flamingo pink with wide celery green stripes. They were a Christmas gift from her L.L.Bean-loving daughter Jennifer, who lived with her snooty husband and three children in the affluent suburb of Tomkins, New Jersey.

There was a peculiar buzz in the air. *Couldn't be June bugs*, Margaret postulated, *those annoying insects won't be making a guest appearance for at least seven or eight months.* She glared at the night sky, trying to pinpoint where the sound was coming from. Margaret's dog Slop, a German Shepherd/English Sheep Dog mix, managed to barrel through the doggie door and sat at attention next to her. She patted the dog's head with her thoroughly callused hands. The tubby pooch perked up at the high-pitched sound, offering up a deep, resonating growl before darting back inside.

Ain't nothin but dang horseflies or some supersonic mosquitoes, probably imported from China. She'd read about those soap bar-sized wasps that could kill a man, livestock too.

The buzzing seemed to be getting closer. Margaret clipped one corner of the fitted sheet with two clothespins then reached down for a couple more. Digging around, she unexpectedly felt a pinch on her middle finger.

"Son of a bitch." She raised her hand staring right at the clothespin. Surprised, she pried it off, noticing blood at the tip of her finger. "You ain't got teeth, do ya?" She paused, assuming it must have been a stupid accident, that's all.

Margaret wiped the blood on her worn jeans. She was about to clip another clothespin to the fitted sheet when she noticed something odd about one of the spring-type wooden clothespins, the only kind Margaret ever used. It seemed to have relocated itself on its own to the edge of the sheet. She always clipped them at least three inches from the edge. Anything less and a stiff breeze could blow 'em right off. The hell she was gonna wash the same sheets twice in one day.

The phone rang. Margaret put the clothespin down and walked back inside to answer the it. She was only gone a minute before she stomped back outside. "Annoying telemarketers," muttered Margaret as she went back to her task at hand.

When she reached the clothesline, she noticed more clothespins lined up on the coated wire. In fact, the whole twenty-five foot stretch of clothesline was filled with them, standing at attention like little wooden soldiers.

"What the dag frick is going on here?" yelled Margaret. She stood still, wondering if she was having a senior moment. Maybe she'd already clipped them on.

That was a crock! Margaret was feisty, quick-witted, and sharp as pitchfork tines. No, something abnormal was going on. Maybe it was one of those stupid ass teens from down the street. She'd had a run-in with a pair of them just last month. Jona and Ginger Gold, twins who lived two houses down, thought dyeing a trio of her treasured snow-white ducks Kelly green for St. Patrick's Day was a good idea. Margaret got her revenge by paint rolling their Toyota Corolla in lipstick pink.

"All right you bunch of zit faces, the gigs up," she said loud and clear. "I gotta gun and I ain't afraid to use it."

Suddenly, she felt an excruciating pinch on the back of her neck.

"Ouch!" She reached around and clutched the perpetrator. "What the . . ." She took out her Bic lighter and examined the culprit clothespin more closely. There was blood around its' . . . "Mouth?" It started to pulsate and glow.

Spooked, she quickly dropped it as if it was a white-hot briquette. Armed with only a pair of worn moccasins, she stomped on it, repeatedly. *How the hell does a clothespin bite?* She was perplexed — unless it was some sort of bizarre government experiment gone array, which she thought could be quite possible.

Margaret heard the buzzing again, whirling like a turbine engine. She felt a weird sensation wiggling under her foot. She stepped aside and peered down. The illuminated little object suddenly torpedoed upward, biting Margaret square on the bridge of her nose.

"Get the hell off me!" she cried in a nasal voice. She pried the clothespin off and threw it towards the woods. The strange buzzing stopped. The forest, usually bursting with the symphony of nature, went deathly silent. Margaret stood still like one of the pine trees in her yard, almost forgetting to breathe. The tip of her finger throbbed. A trickle of blood dripped from her injured snout.

All at once, they ravaged the woman, biting her all over her stumpy body, attacking like a ferocious school of piranhas, relentless to the core. They darted in and out, biting Margaret repeatedly, now bloodied and wounded. She tried fending them off, but her motions were too slow. Decades of manual labor made her limbs sluggish and achy. She fell to the ground onto the worn grass. She couldn't stop them, not now, nor for the next hour. The clothespins began pulsating into a highlighter yellow glow as they absorbed her blood. In a flash, the cluster of clothespins vanished leaving Margaret's body lying on the ground.

Chapter 2

The next morning, Bob Cortland, all-purpose electrician and horseshoe-tossing champion of Red Orchard, New York, arrived at Margaret's farmhouse. Usually she'd be out there to greet him on the front porch with a spare cup of Joe. Occasionally, on good weather afternoons, the two would get together at the Rotten Core Pub on the outskirts of town, consuming adult beverages and dining on burgers the size of shuffleboard disks.

Bob stepped out of his truck carrying his toolbox, a jelly donut securely planted in his mouth. His stout New Year's resolution of not consuming donuts anymore had lasted a mere seventy-two hours. He loved jelly donuts. He walked up to the white-trimmed painted screen door and knocked.

"Margie, you home?" Bob called out, wiping the powdered sugar on his jacket sleeve. No answer. He noticed her apple red Ford F150 was parked in the driveway. He knocked again, calling out her name a bit louder. Slop trotted out from the kitchen to the screen door, his nails tatting on the hard oak wood surface. The dog began shifting back and forth nervously, barking up a storm.

"It's okay Slop, it's okay. Where's the boss?" The dog made a sudden rush and thrust the screen door open, running around the house to the back yard. Cortland placed his beat-up Sears Craftsman toolbox down on the front step and followed. He spotted the dog near the clothesline, sitting anxiously by Margaret's lifeless body.

"Oh Christ no," said Bob. He rushed over, figuring it was a heart attack – probably popped an artery yelling at some trespassers – that or the pounds of succulent pork products she consumed on a weekly basis that had finally done her in. Then he saw the blood.

"What in God's name?" Bob wiped his hand across his suddenly dry mouth in horror. There were dozens of flesh wounds on her back, maybe hundreds of them. Cortland stood up and surveyed the woods. He trembled.

"Cops – gotta call the cops." The cell phone reception was genuinely horrendous in Margaret's neck of the woods, but he tried anyway. The phone rang. A female voice answered, fading in and out with a snap, crackle, pop.

"Holly, it's me, Bob Cortland. Is Sheriff Taylor there? I gotta get a hold of him, pronto. Margaret Braeburn's been attacked – murdered!"

"Mean Margaret, dead?" replied Holly. "When, where?"

"I just found her body, face down at her house in the back yard. Something attacked her – there's blood all over the place!"

"Stay right there, Bob. I'll call the sheriff right away. He's at the Devil's Donut right now. Supposedly a fight broke out between customers, probably bikers again."

"Just tell him to get up here ASAP!"

Bob hung up. He tried to avoid looking at Margaret's dead body, but couldn't. Stuff like this never happen in the quaint upstate town. An impulsive wave of fear suddenly blanketed the portly electrician. Maybe there's a homicidal maniac on the prowl lurking in the dark woods. He raced back to his car and locked the doors.

He glanced at his watch. "Come on, where are you!" Nineteen minutes later, the sheriff showed up, lights flashing.

Sheriff Taylor, still in solid shape for a man turning sixty-four, pulled up next to Bob's pickup and got out of his car. Bob did too; still in shock, his legs were weak and rubbery. "Hi Sheriff."

"Mike to you. We're friends remember?"

"I know, I know, sorry – just doing the respect thing." Bob took in a deep breath.

The sheriff zipped up his jacket; it was always chillier up in the hills. "Where is she?"

"In the back yard, by the clothesline. I still can't believe it."

Both men walked around towards the back yard. "You said Margie was murdered? How do you know?" Sheriff Taylor turned away from Bob and laid eyes on the body.

"Holy Grail." The sheriff moved in closer, inspecting not only the body, but also the surroundings. "You didn't touch anything, did you?"

"No, nothing, I swear." Bob took off his Cincinnati Reds baseball cap, wiping his brow. "What the hell could have done this?"

"It might have been some animal, but I don't recognize this type of bite wound, not at all. Hold on." The sheriff took out a pen and brushed aside a piece of Margaret's tattered flannel shirt.

"Is that a clothespin? The two looked at each other, puzzled. "Lend me a hand." The sheriff and Bob carefully turned the body over to reveal Margaret's half-eaten face. A handful more that were still feasting on her bulbous midsection rocketed away.

Bob fainted on cue; the sheriff was not too far behind.

Chapter 3

At a secluded lake miles from the nearest anything, two men, retirees from Queens, New York, gently paddled along in their matte green Old Town fiberglass canoe. The pristine lake, still as ice, reflected the autumn leaves like a joyous fall postcard. From above, the center of the roundish body of water appeared much darker, like a blot of ink. The two were former postal employees and childhood friends, having survived thirty years of banal mail delivery and the elements of the big city: rain, sleet, snow, heat, and abusive city folks. Both men and their wives had enjoyed spending occasional long weekend retreats upstate, thriving on the peace and tranquility of Red Orchard before moving there permanently last year when both men finally called it quits.

The sun penetrating through the late afternoon clouds made temperatures near ideal. Occasionally, they'd hit a cool spot where the temperature seemed to drop ten degrees, making them shiver. The two took a break, coasting gently on the darkened water as they devoured on matching baloney sandwiches, complete with yellow mustard and yellow American cheese, just like in grade school. Thirsty, one of the men popped open a couple of chilled Wailing Wenches, a dark amber ale brewed locally in nearby Syracuse – definitely NOT like grade school.

"Man, this stuff is good," boasted Tom Arlet, slender and in respectable shape, a year older than his heavier friend Rich Alexander. "And to think you wanted to bring a Pepsi."

"You know I'm not real keen on drinking while fishing," replied Rich. "I get buzzed and end up hooking my finger or something stupid. Remember last time?"

"It's a prerequisite to fish and drink, and not necessarily in that order my friend," answered Tom. "Why the hell else would we be out here?"

"We like to fish, don't we?" answered Rich.

"Of course we do, but when I'm catching nothing, which is most of the time lately, I like to kick back and enjoy an ice cold *cervesa*, as they say in Spanish."

Tom tipped his hat, smiling. He baited his hook with a half-cut nightcrawler and cast out his line. The red-and-white bobber splashed down on the water like the Apollo 13 spacecraft, creating a mild ripple.

Rich did the same, but managed to target a fallen, protruding branch. "Shit." He slammed down his son's economy model Zebco 404 rod-and-reel combo. Exasperated, Tom handed his friend a beer. Rich took a sniff, savoring the fine scent like a vintage bottle of wine, then took a healthy gulp. "Thank God for beer."

"Ale," corrected Tom. "We're drinking ale."

"What difference does it make, as long as it's got the big A, am I right? A as in alcohol. And this stuff's got almost eight percent: jeeze Louise I'm gonna be a drunken mess!"

Tom smirked. "You sound like Sesame Street for God's sake . . . A is for alcohol. And B is for bite! I think I've got one!"

A buzzing sound emanated from the trees.

"Hold on, you hear that?" asked Rich. Cicadas, maybe? His friend was too preoccupied with his pending catch.

"Man-o-man, this feels like a large mouth for sure," crowed Tom, hoping the eight-pound test would hold up. "Look at my pole for Christ sake; it's bending like a U!"

Rich rested his paddle across the canoe and looked deep into the encompassing woods. He'd heard many a sound on his numerous vacations to upstate Red Orchard, but this was different, almost like a whining blender.

Tom continued to battle the fish, now close to the canoe. "He's gone under the boat. Quick, hand me the net – quickly before it breaks my freaking line!"

Rich reached behind his seat cushion and picked up the short-handled, green aluminum nylon net. "Here."

The fish fought like crazy, twisting and twirling in the brisk water, creating a foamy, chilled froth. Tom snagged the great fish and hoisted it in the net, proud as a peacock. "I got you, you son a bitch!"

Tom was in fishing bliss, his beaming smile almost hurting his face. "This sucker's gotta be over twenty inches long!"

The clothespins jettison from the myriad of trees, hundreds and hundreds of them. They attacked the two men like flying barracudas. The feisty bass disappeared right before Tom's eyes as they shredded it to pieces. "Hey, my fish!"

That's when the two felt the painful bites. The sky above the canoe darkened as the swarm of clothespins attacked the two men. Rich tried to curl up in a ball, pushing his head between his knees for protection, but he was too doughy and exposed. They chomped at the easy target, blood now flowing from the multiple wounds. He wailed in pain as they tore him to pieces.

Tom brandished the chewed-up aluminum net like a weekend tennis player, swatting at anything that zigged or zagged, occasionally hitting the target.

Dozens went for his bearded face, drawing blood quickly around his ears and neck. He frantically waved the net but soon tired. He tried to reposition himself in the canoe but lost his balance, spilling into the lake. Tom raised his tattered arms, desperately trying to swim freestyle to shore. More clothespins zeroed in on his broad back like seagulls descending upon a floating dead whale. He tired quickly before descending below the surface like a dropped brick. In a matter of seconds, he was out of view in the murky water.

Rich was dead too, still balled up on the floor of the canoe. Blood mixed with the thin layer of omnipresent lake water, turning it a light red hue. The canoe floated aimlessly towards a half sunken tree where it finally nestled in between two outreaching branches like skeletal limbs.

Chapter 4

Near dinnertime and halfway out the door, Holly heard the phone ring. For a split second she thought of brushing it off, but she was a professional. Besides, her replacement was pulling into the parking lot. She trekked back inside, grabbing the phone on the fourth ring.

"Red Orchard Police, how can I help you?"

'Uh, hi." The young man's voice was nervous and squeaky.

"Yes, may I help you?" Holly's stomach grumbled in hunger for the umpteenth time. God, she hated dieting.

"Um, my friend and I are biking out here at Crispin Lake and we see a canoe all by itself on the water; sort of strange. There's an empty car in the parking lot too; it might belong to them, but there's no one here."

"Thank you, I'll have someone stop by and take a look. And your name, sir?" The man abruptly hung up. He and his friend had just finished up a fat joint and were closing in on the paranoid/munchie stage. They weren't about to divulge any more information than they had to.

Holly radioed the boss, who was finishing up a couple of slices of pizza and a Coke at Melinda's Italian restaurant. "What can I do for you?" Sheriff Taylor grimaced as he noticed a quarter-size sauce stain on his new jacket. He quickly wiped it off.

"Someone just called about an empty canoe floating around on Crispin Lake," said Holly.

The sheriff replied with a mouthful of pizza topped with green peppers and onion. "I'm on my way."

Sheriff Taylor, got there just as the sun dissipated behind a line of towering pines. He pulled into the parking lot, noticing the lone vehicle. The sheriff took out a thick yellow nylon rope from the trunk and followed the recycled plastic walkway leading to the lake. The canoe had drifted free of the branches, now floating fifteen-plus feet from the end of the protruding dock. The sheriff was in no mood to get wet. Hell, after reading about people contracting flesh-eating viruses from lakes, he wasn't about to take any chances either.

He trekked back off the dock and found a thick branch. He broke it in half over his knee and tied the smaller piece to the rope as a weight. He sauntered back to the end of the dock but stopped momentarily, hearing a strange humming sound coming from the forest. He positioned himself next to one of the pylons and swung the rope back and forth to get some momentum.

The sheriff's first toss clanked off the bow, gently moving the canoe into deeper water. "Damn it." The sheriff hastily tried again as the canoe shifted, this time landing just inside the center of the craft. "All right now."

He began towing in the canoe when he heard buzzing again, only this time it was louder. The canoe was almost within reach. He bent down on one knee and spotted a couple of seat cushions, fishing pole, cooler, and dark-tinted water on the floor. Then a man's body appeared, curled up, mangled, and bloodied.

"Oh God, not another." The sheriff pulled the boat ashore through the tall grass and mud, then paused, surveying the horrific scene. It was getting dark now. The buzzing sound intensified. He grabbed the flashlight from his belt and shined it at the trees.

Sheriff Taylor marched back to his car and called the station. "Holly? Oh, hi Paula, I guess she finally went home."

"Yeah, Holly just left. Said she was craving a cheeseburger deluxe from Granny's Diner."

"So much for her diet, I guess," said the sheriff. "Look, this has been a horrible day and it just got worse. I need the medical examiner out here at Crispin Lake right away. There's been another attack."

The sheriff hung up and ran the license plate of the SUV. He followed it up, eventually contacting the spouses and learning that there were two people out there fishing.

He called back. "Paula, contact Deputy Stearns and tell him to bring his scuba equipment. We may have another dead body somewhere in the lake."

Chapter 5

The Baldwin parents finally gave their children Brian and Maggie, ages eleven and nine, permission to set up their very own tent, a birthday present for their son last week, and camp out in the back yard. It was fenced in so they felt at ease. The two children, dressed in sweatpants and sweatshirts, relocated their stuffed animal collection, books, and a battery-operated Coleman lantern into the four-man bright green tent. Maggie snuggled into her rosy pink Hello Kitty sleeping bag with her three-foot stuffed animal dolphin, reading *The World According to Humphry*. Brian snuck a box of salty Goldfish snacks and buried his head into *The Zombie Survival Guide*, his new favorite book – *Goosebumps* was so yesterday. He brought along an oversized bright yellow-and-blue beach towel for added warmth.

Mom and Dad came outside near nine PM to check on the kids. "So far, so good," both Brian and Maggie reported, signaling with a big thumbs up.

"We'll leave the back door open if you need anything, okay?" said Mom. The children nodded and continued with their backyard adventure. They noshed and read, but then the yawns started coming, one after the other.

Hours later, Brian's glowing Timex watch beeped. It was midnight, and both children were sound asleep. Maggie, inheritor of Mom's light sleeping habits, awoke. There were muffled tapping sounds all along the tent, slight at first but persistent. She could see peculiar movements all around the tent, like someone poking their index finger haphazardly along the thin fabric. She heard a buzzing, deep at first, before revving into high gear.

Maggie called for her brother, but he didn't respond. Brian, like Dad, slept like a slab of cement. The jabbing continued, all around the tent. Maggie burrowed deep inside her sleeping bag. Then she felt something nipping outside at her toes. It was moving nearer, inching its way towards her. A rat, maybe? The buzzing sound was getting closer to her face. Maggie continued to huddle under and didn't move a muscle. After what seemed like forever, she stuck her head out slowly like a shelled-up turtle. Her dark brown eyes peeked out.

The clothespin darted straight for her. It bit down hard on her shoulder length brown hair, nicking her ear. Maggie screamed. Brian, full-fledged groggy, finally woke up. "What's the problem – I was sound asleep!"

Maggie's screams seemed to excite the clothespins outside. "What the heck is happening?" he exclaimed.

Maggie was bleeding. "Sis!" The clothespin suddenly lunged at Brian. He lifted up his forearm to block the flying object, but it bit him hard just below the elbow. He cried out in pain. "Mommy, help!"

The children's cries awoke Mrs. Baldwin. She quickly ran outside, towards the tent.

"Get in, get in, hurry!" urged Brian.

Mrs. Baldwin got on her hands and knees and crawled inside and zipped it up. Mom saw the blood running down her daughter's head and down Brian's arm. "You're bleeding. What's going on?"

"I don't know, but I trapped it – whatever it is." The clothespin was glowing, fighting to escape.

Dad appeared at the back door. "Is everything alright?" he called. He saw the bizarre cloud of clothespins now hovering over the tent. "Oh my God, stay still, I'll be right back."

Mr. Baldwin scrambled to get the fire extinguisher tucked under the kitchen sink. He grabbed the thick, hand-knit wool blanket resting on the living room sofa to use as a shield.

"Stay put until I get there!" he yelled. He ran into the yard spraying the fire extinguisher in the air as he sprinted over to the tent. The cold, cloudlike mist temporarily confused the clothespins; a few even dropped from the air. The family burst out from the tent and huddled under the blanket. They scurried back into the house and locked the door.

Dad raced upstairs and downstairs, making sure every window was closed shut. He double-checked the chimney flue then peered out the backyard window. Mom took the children to the bathroom to clean up their wounds.

"I think we're okay, Jen," said Mr. Baldwin. He picked up the phone and called the sheriff's office. "What are those things?"

Brian went into the laundry room and found an empty peanut butter jar. He managed to force the clothespin into the container. The boy sealed it tight and gazed at the snapping wooden object, the pulsating animated glow now fading.

Maggie turned on her cat-faced toy flashlight that she'd won at the town carnival last year. "It looks like one of mom's clippies."

"This is really weird," added Brian.

"Red Orchard Police, Deputy Thomas Monroe speaking."

"Hello deputy? This is William Baldwin at 25 Tydeman Street. Sorry I'm calling so late, but our children were just attacked by something in our back yard."

"Attacked? By what, a raccoon, feral cat?"

"They're clippies, Dad," said Maggie as she tugged at her dad's favorite blue terry cloth robe.

"Not quite," replied Mr. Baldwin. The kids chimed in loud and clear. "They're clippies – those things mommy uses on the clothesline!" Brian held up the jar containing the lone specimen, pushing it near Dad's face.

"I'm sorry deputy; they're clippies." Dad turned to his kids, not believing what he was saying.

"Could you please spell that for me," asked the deputy patiently.

"Uh, hold on for moment. "Kids, do I spell that with a YS or IES?"

The children looked at each other. "IES?"

"C-l-i-p-p-i-e-s. They look kind of like – well actually, they're . . . clothespins."

"You're saying your children were attacked by clothespins, am I right?"

"Uh, yes."

"Killer clothespins?"

"Apparently so," replied Mr. Baldwin. "Look, I know this is about as strange as it gets, but . . ."

"Mr. Baldwin, prior to becoming a deputy I worked the graveyard shift at BuyMart so I know strange, but killer clothespins? That's off the charts." The deputy paused then sighed. "Give me twenty minutes. Stay put and don't go outside hanging up any laundry, promise?"

"We promise." Mr. Baldwin hung up the phone.

"So?" asked his wife.

"He'll be over in about twenty minutes, but I'm fairly certain he thinks we're smoking the hippy lettuce."

Chapter 6

Deputy Monroe hung up the phone and tipped his hat to Paula. "I'm off to the Baldwin house – got a killer clothespin situation to take care of, be right back."

Paula offered up a puzzled look then smiled, batting her awning-like natural eyelashes. "Be safe, my hero." The heavy-set deputy giggled as he left the building. He had a crush on her and was always so close to asking her out on a date, but continually chickened out again and again. *One of these days.*

The deputy got in his car and followed Cottonmouth Road, a nightmarish stretch of pavement with more twists and turns than a rollercoaster. Flashes of light made the deputy shield his eyes with his hand. "Man, that was . . ." He suddenly jammed on the brakes, almost hitting the object. His hat toppled off his head, striking the windshield.

Monroe gathered his wits and turned on the hazard lights before stepping out of the Ford Explorer with his flashlight. The screeching tire smoke mixed with the high beams, creating an eerie, pungent fog. He'd seen this before, a dead deer lying square on the double yellow lines. There was a lot of blood, probably a truck had clobbered the poor animal.

As the deputy stepped closer, he noticed movement, twitching was more like it, all along the carcass. He pinpointed the flashlight beam on the midsection and inched closer, crouching down on one knee. *No way.*

111

"Oh, this is messed up." Hundreds of glowing clippies gnashed away at the carcass, each digging into the flesh. The deputy stared in disbelief at the feeding frenzy. He gagged then coughed.

All at once, the clippies stopped munching. The deputy continued to stand there like a statue, still angling his flashlight at the deer. One particular clippie gnawing on the deer's snout creaked its little wood frame and shot straight at Monroe, grazing the right side of the deputy's face like a stray bullet. The deputy felt a warm sensation. He raised the tip of his fingers and touched blood. Stunned, he dropped the flashlight and ran for the car.

All at once, half the clippies jettison from the dead animal and began their assault. Monroe waved his arms frantically trying to escape the swarm. He tripped, falling to his knees. He rose, desperate to crawl back to the car. More clothespins whistled through the dense, charcoal gray sky, a whirlwind of darting flying objects. He screamed as they pecked at his hands and lower legs. A few managed to dig under his official Red Orchard Police jacket. One latched on to his earlobe, left unprotected by his hat. A handful snapped at his blubbery love handles, left exposed by the undersized jacket. With every ounce of strength, the deputy finally pulled himself up, opened the door, and tumbled inside the car.

"Holy mother of God!" He quickly shut the door and started the car. He felt a pinching sensation on the back of his neck. More were still attached to the jacket like sand spurs to beach sandals, all in a frenzied hunt for human flesh. In a cumbersome fashion, he stripped off his jacket and then rolled down the window, tossing it outside. Monroe barehanded the ones attached to his neck like ticks before speeding off.

The deputy finally pulled up the Baldwin's driveway and slammed on the brakes, getting as close as possible to the front door. He paused for a moment, trying to regroup after the startling assault. His police issued attire had protected a good portion of his portly body. Most of the wounds were to his hands, neck and ears. His gut would've been fine if it weren't for the jacket being one size too small.

Monroe staggered to the front door, still trying to catch his breath, and rang the bell multiple times.

A woman dressed in gray sweatpants and a blue Buffalo Bills sweatshirt answered the door.

"Mrs. Baldwin?"

"Yes?"

"You're not crazy after all." The deputy stepped inside before collapsing on the carpeted floor.

Chapter 7

A half hour later, Monroe was alert, bruised but bandaged, and sitting upright in the kitchen chair drinking a tall glass of orange juice. He borrowed the phone and called Sheriff Mike Taylor at his home.

"Hey boss. My apologies for calling you so late but–"

"No problem, Deputy." Monroe could tell he just woke him up. "What's news?"

"I'm up at the Baldwin residence. We've got ourselves a killer clothespin situation." The Baldwin parents corrected him. "Sorry, killer clippies – and they're freaking everywhere! They almost killed me tonight. They swarm like those African killer bees. We gotta warn the town!" There was silence at the other end. "Sheriff?"

"You're absolutely positive, deputy? Killer . . . clippies?"

"I swear," said Monroe, staring at the multiple bandages on his hands.

"I'll meet you at the station," said the sheriff, bleary-eyed and achy. "We may need to contact the local radio station to start spreading the news. Fifteen minutes, deputy."

The deputy turned to the Baldwin parents. "Folks, I want you to stay indoors, don't open any windows, and call your neighbors to warn them. These things are lethal, okay?"

"You got it," replied Mr. Baldwin.

Chapter 8

Residents from all over Red Orchard were ringing up the police station. Paula Redd, three months new as the night shift dispatcher, needed to be an octopus to pick up all the calls. The effervescent thirty-two year-old brunette originally took the night shift to pay the bills and fund her return to school, figuring it would be a cinch. That was not the case tonight.

Sheriff Taylor arrived at the station, tired and cranky.

"What the hell is going on tonight, Sheriff?" asked Paula. "The phones have been ringing non-stop! Something about big insects going haywire."

"Well, according to Deputy Monroe, the town of Red Orchard is under siege by clippies."

"Clippies?" asked Paula. "What the hell are clippies?"

"You know – those things you use to hang up your clothes on."

"You mean clothespins? Citizens are being attacked by clothespins?"

"As bizarre as it may sound, these clippies have apparently killed three people, maybe more."

Deputy Monroe came busting through the door sporting multiple bandages plastered across his ears, hands, and a large one behind his neck. There was even a bright yellow SpongeBob Band Aid adhered across the bridge of his nose.

"Holy crap, what the hell happened to you?" asked Paula. She rushed over and helped the deputy sit down in one of the lobby chairs.

"Are you okay," said Taylor. "Maybe you should go home and rest. We can handle –"

"No, you can't, Mike, not this," said Monroe. "These things are everywhere. I got a call that a bunch more people were attacked at White Castle. What happened at Crispin Lake, did Walters find the other body?"

"Yeah," replied the sheriff, pouring himself a cup of coffee. "Said the guy looked like he'd been shredded by piranhas – it was horrible."

"Well, what do we do now?" asked Monroe. "We've got no chance!"

"We've got put our heads together on this one," said Paula. Taylor and Monroe looked at her. "When did all this start happening?"

"I guess last night – with Margie," replied the sheriff as he rubbed his chin.

"Well, the meteor shower began last night, right? And what if that meteor shower, I don't know, somehow reacted with the metal on each of the clothespins?" suggested Paula.

"Oh jeeze," sighed Taylor. He started whistling the *X-Files* theme.

"You're a sci-fi geek too?" grinned Monroe, his brain percolating now with possible theories. Paula smiled back. He was a voracious reader of science fiction, mostly Orson Scott Card, H.G. Wells, and Ray Bradbury. "Maybe you got something there."

Paula started pacing back and forth, Monroe joined in, albeit with a slight limp.

"Okay, enough Muldoon and Scully," said the sheriff. "We need something a bit more tangible here."

Monroe politely corrected his boss. "It's Mulder, not Muldoon."

Taylor gave the deputy an icy stare. "What we need to do now is . . ." He stopped talking, hearing a peculiar noise.

A sudden high-pitched buzz engulfed what seemed like the whole downtown square. The three shuffled to the front glass double door, amazed by its intensity.

Taylor zeroed in, his nose almost touching against the glass. He cupped each side of his eyes. Out in the distance, he spotted something that resembled fireflies.

Monroe shifted his size twelve feet on over and peered out. He turned pale as vanilla ice cream. "It's them."

"What is it?" asked Paula. "Tommy, are you alright"?

The sheriff remained still. "Quiet; both of you." Taylor peered deeper through the glass. He opened the door halfway and stepped outside. He barely had time to dart back in.

The clothespins pelted the front door like a relentless hailstorm. From every direction the clippies bombarded the one-story building. Hundreds pressed against the door like fish trying to escape a trolling net, pushing at the door until it started opening. They kept coming, hitting the glass like thrown rocks, each time harder than the last.

Paula rushed over, helping her co-workers to lock it. All three took a step back.

Deputy Monroe was sweating bullets, his heart racing. "This door better hold, or we're toast."

"We should be okay," said Sheriff, "It's bulletproof."

Chapter 9

The clippies continued their assault on the building.

"How's the door situation looking?" asked Monroe.

"It's holding so far, but I'm not taking any chances," said Taylor, who had started layering every open crevice with duct tape. "Those little evil bastards don't give up." Sheriff Taylor had already put in a full day. And despite consuming a half-gallon of coffee, his eyelids were sagging. The only thing keeping him awake was the frequent treks to the bathroom.

"So, what do we know so far?" asked Paula, searching feverishly for an answer. "The light shower seemed to provide the necessary energy. As long as these meteor showers continue . . ."

"We're screwed is what you're saying," said Monroe, who, like Paula, enjoyed the peace and tranquility to working the night shift.

"After all this is over, what do you say you and I have dinner and see a movie?" asked Paula.

"Uh – I'd like that really much, I mean very much," the deputy replied, blushing. "I know a great new horror – "

"Let's put the horror movies on hiatus for time being, okay?" asked Paula. "And absolutely no chick flicks either. I'd rather bathe in barbeque sauce and stand outside with those clippies than watch that stuff."

"Ugh, how gross," said Monroe.

Taylor returned from the bathroom and walked over to the front door. The clippies were still swarming the building, tap, tap, tap like snare drums, as they continued to peck at the glass. "At least we're safe for now – oh no."

"Oh no, what?" asked Monroe.

Sheriff Taylor gazed up at the ceiling noticing particles of tiles falling like snowflakes. There was a buzzing sound coming from above. "Don't anybody move."

"They're inside?" asked Paula, anxiously looking at her boss.

"Apparently so." Taylor eyed his co-worker. "Paula, grab the fire extinguisher behind you, but no sudden moves, okay?"

Paula backed up against the wall and opened the plastic handled door and picked up the extinguisher. "You do know this thing expired like two years ago."

"It'll be fine. They're like Twinkies, they'll last forever," replied the sheriff.

"I'll get the one in the kitchen too," said Monroe.

Taylor motioned to the deputy. "Good."

Monroe tiptoed down the hallway towards the kitchen, keeping an eye on the ceiling. Unfortunately, he wasn't as graceful as Paula, tripping over a metal trashcan. Clank. The buzzing stopped. A handful of clippies burst through shooting directly at Paula.

"Now!" yelled Taylor.

Paula let loose with the extinguisher. The blasting cold met the descending clippies head on. Monroe raced to the kitchen and grabbed the other extinguisher from under the sink and stormed back, returning fire. Half of the clippies dropped to the ground, but others quickly engulfed Paula.

"Get them off me, get them off me!"

Monroe showered Paula with an icy blast, coating her white as snow. More clippies dropped to the linoleum floor like dead insects. The rest vanished in a heartbeat, retreating through the ceiling vent. "It's working, it's working!" screamed Monroe. "Take that you little shits – no one messes with my woman!"

The sheriff ran back to his office and retrieved a roll of bright orange duct tape, a mainstay in any police station. He positioned a step stool under the vent and began ripping off strip after strip, blocking the narrow openings.

"Sweep those up things and put 'em in the safe, quickly," said Taylor. "We can't risk opening the door and tossing them outside."

"I think the cold stuns them, but only momentarily," said Monroe, who put down the spent container and grabbed the broom and dustpan from the closet. As he swept, he could see the clippies regaining movement. "Oh, Shih Tzu."

"Jeeze, where'd you learn to sweep?" asked Paula. "Felix Unger, you're not."

Monroe looked up at Paula and snickered. "I've got a better idea; you take care of this and I'll unlock the safe."

The deputy grabbed the key from the sheriff and headed to the seldom-used second office in the back. He entered the dusty room and slid some boxes aside. He bent down on one knee and opened the safe with the key and called out. "I'm all set here."

Paula finished sweeping the handful of clippies and jogged over to the storage room where she tossed them in. Satisfied, she closed the metal door. "Got 'em locked up in the pokey. Now what?"

***

Bob Cortland couldn't sleep, tossing and turning for hours. The horror of seeing Margie dead like that, mauled by inanimate objects, was too much for him to handle. He still couldn't believe it. What the hell could be more harmless than a clothespin? It was completely surreal, like some B-horror nightmare.

Bob finally dragged his body out of bed. He dressed in his familiar red-checkered flannel shirt and dark blue Levi jeans then headed downstairs into the kitchen. He took out a slice of leftover pepperoni pizza from the refrigerator and poured himself a glass of ginger ale.

After his midnight snack, Bob slipped on his duck boots, grabbed the car keys, and walked into the garage. There in a corner, he picked up a vintage Wilson T-2000 tennis racquet, the kind Jimmy Connors used to kick ass with back in the day. He grasped the dusty relic for protection and opened the garage door.

The night air was crisp and cool, just the way he liked it. Bob got into his beast of a truck, a mammoth eight-cylinder, top-of-the-line, black Dodge Ram 3500 four door. He pressed on the gas and shot out of the driveway. Bob wasn't exactly sure where to go, but felt like he had to do something; the Red Orchard Police Station seemed like a good place to start.

Chapter 10

Both Paula and Monroe walked down the hallway feeling upbeat when the ceiling tiles above exploded in pieces. In seconds, hundreds of clippies swarmed the 6,000 square-foot station.

"Holy Christ!" yelled Sheriff Taylor. The three ran towards the front lobby and grabbed seat cushions for protection. A truck pulled up near the front entrance.

A loud horn blared.

"Who's that?" asked Monroe, glancing out the window.

"Who cares," screamed Paula. "Let's run for it!"

"On three," screamed Taylor.

"We don't have till three; run your ass off!" yelled Monroe, trying to be heard over the intense turbine roar.

Bob Cortland rolled down the side window a couple of inches. "Hurry, hurry!" He leaned over and opened the front and back passenger doors.

The three dove into the truck. A few clippies managed to trail inside, but Taylor scooped them up and threw them out the window. "You, my friend, are a life saver," said the sheriff, out of breath."

"Life savers is more like it," added Monroe, sweating. As Bob pulled out the parking lot, Sheriff Taylor asked him why he was out so late.

"I couldn't sleep, Mike," replied Cortland, agitated. "Not after what happened to Margie. I felt like I had to do something."

"Well, your timing is impeccable. Thank you," added Paula, giving the man a pat on the shoulder.

"So, what's our next move, folks?" asked Cortland.

"The cold seems to stun them, but not for long," said Monroe. "Other than that, I believe the town of Red Orchard is up a certain creek without a paddle."

"I think the key to this whole thing is tied to the meteor shower," said Paula. "That's their power source!"

"I think I got something," said Bob, the mechanisms in his brain churning. "These things are just stinking clothespins, right?"

"Yeah," replied the sheriff. "So?"

"And what do clothespins generally do – I mean when they're not killing people?" The other three sat in silence. "Come on, this ain't rocket science." He egged them on.

"Uh . . . hold up . . . clothes?" uttered Monroe.

"Exactly!" boasted Cortland. "So what if we create a super long clothesline out of metal wire, I mean a hundred yards long if we have to, and I run a charge to my big badass Interstate battery? We get them to clip on, and then I'll shock those little shits back to reality. They need to get back to what they're supposed to do, and that's holding up laundry, not eating people."

"Works for me," said Monroe.

Paula shrugged her shoulders. "Why not?"

"And what do we use as bait – us?" asked the sheriff.

Bob thought for a moment. "I don't know, how about a red sheet?"

"Or maybe a big T-bone steak?" jested Monroe.

"If this works, I'm making you an honorary deputy," said Taylor.

"And if it fails, we're making you honorary scapegoat," joked Monroe. Paula elbowed him.

"Sorry. I thought humor was always a good thing when you're stressing. And I'm stressing."

"My shop is just around the corner. I got enough wire to encircle the entire town of Red Orchard. We go there, get some supplies, and then head to the high school. I'll wrap a line around the goal posts, and let my battery do the rest."

As Bob pulled up to the back entrance to his shop, a whole congregation of clippies hovered above the truck like a storm cloud. He laid on the horn, startling them momentarily. "Look at 'em," he said before flicking on the wipers on high, swatting more away to clear his view.

"It's like a freaking snowstorm!" added the deputy.

"I'm gonna run inside real quick, okay?"

"You need any help?" asked the sheriff, flinching his eyes as clippies pelted the window.

"No, I need all of you to stay right here, it'll be easier for me to do this solo." Cortland turned off the motor and prepared to jump out. "Be back in ten minutes. Sheriff, lay on the horn."

Bob thrusts open the door and ran over to the rear entrance, his key already out, ready to open the lock. By the time the startled clippies prepared to attack, Bob was already inside.

Less than fifteen minutes later, Bob emerged carrying a large wooden spool of wire and a small black duffle bag of supplies slung over his shoulder. The sheriff laid on the horn again then propped the door open for the electrician. Bob shot inside and slammed the door shut, breaking a handful of sneaking clippies.

"Okay, I've got the wire and even found an old red towel we can hang for bait."

"Why a towel?" asked Monroe.

"I don't know, maybe they're attracted to red garments – like sharks to blood.

"You're shirt's red, Bob" said Paula. "Maybe you should change?"

Bob scoffed. "I'll be fine. As for the plan, we can attach some of the dead clippies to the wire and use them as decoys." He felt energized, smart as a tack. He backed out of the parking lot and sped away towards the high school.

Bob reached the entrance then headed for the football field. "Last thing we need do is turn on the lights and make some noise. That should attract them for sure." He followed the curving side road until reaching the chain link fence. It was locked.

"Shit, and we don't have a key."

"Is there another entrance?" asked Paula.

"No, this is it," replied Bob. "Sheriff, will you vouch for me if my insurance refuses to cover the damages to my truck?"

"You're vouched."

Bob backed up then floored the gas pedal, barreling right through the fence like a bruising running back. He rolled onto the pristine grass football field doing thirty-five miles per hour and headed for the opposing goal post.

"He's at the fifty, the forty, the –"

"Not now, deputy," instructed Taylor.

Bob slammed on the brakes, skidding on the slick, low cut turf. He parked the truck just under the goal post and turned to Monroe. "Give me that wire."

"Damn this is heavy," said the deputy as he handed over the wood spool from the back seat.

Bob scanned the night sky. All clear. "Okay folks, this should only take a second."

He jumped out of the truck then climbed up to the back of the pickup. He wrapped the wire around the center crossbar ten feet off the ground and twisted and tightened the end with wire cutters then rushed back holding the spool under his brawny arm, handing it to the sheriff. Seconds later, the first clippies appeared.

"Damn it," said Monroe.

"No, no, we need 'em to return – just not all at once," replied Bob, who placed a thick dowel in the middle of the spool before handing it to the sheriff. "Okay now, just make sure the wire doesn't get tangled up."

Bob got back inside the truck and put the truck in drive. He paced himself, doing ten miles per hour as the fire fed from the spool. "How's it going?"

"No issues," said Taylor.

Bob approached the opposing end zone, backing up under the goalpost. "Alright, hand me the wire cutters."

"Be careful," said Paula.

Bob got out of the truck and headed to the other side as Taylor handed him the lightened spool. He tossed it in the bed of the truck then struggled to climb up. He took the wire cutters from his back pocket and cut the wire to the appropriate length. Bob wrapped the wire around the other goal post and twisted it tight. He cut off another piece of wire, attached it to the goal post, then ran it to the battery. He popped the hood and started hooking up the connection.

"How much longer?" asked Monroe.

Sheriff Taylor looked at the time – it was past three in the morning. No wonder he felt like he was going to collapse.

"Almost done," said Bob as he continued working feverishly, nipping his index finger by accident in the process. He contoured the wire and was about to attach one end of the jumper cables when he heard the familiar buzz. Bob turned around just as the swarm of clippies attacked. All three shuttered as he cried for help.

"Stay here, Paula," ordered Taylor. The sheriff and deputy jumped out immediately and ran over to Bob. He flailed his arms trying to defend himself. The two picked him off the ground and dragged him inside the truck. Paula reached up and grabbed a trio of clothespins from the collar of Bob's jacket and held them in a vice grip.

Monroe handed her a strip of duct tape and corralled them like little bandits.

"I'm all right. Thank you both," huffed Bob. Paula used the red towel to wipe the blood off the multiple wounds. "There's something else I need to do."

"What's that?" asked Paula.

"Place the towel on the line, and . . ."

"And what?" asked Monroe.

"Just give me a second folks," said Bob, barely able to get the words out. "I just need to catch my breath. I haven't done much running since the grand opening of that 'all you can eat' barbeque joint in town," he said with a half smile.

"Take your time," replied Paula.

"You gotta turn on the sprinkler system and then fasten the jumper cables. When I turn on the juice, the water should add a shocking punch." He coughed, gazing at his injured hands.

"You're not going anywhere," said Paula.

"How are we going to hang up the towel?" inquired Monroe. "You can't move the truck now that it's ready to go."

"Good point," replied Bob, his hands throbbing in pain now. "Someone's gonna have to run to midfield, drape it on the line and secure it, and run back. I don't think I'm in any condition – "

"You've already done enough – I'll do it," said Paula.

"Tell me where the sprinkler system is and I'll take care of that end of it," said the sheriff.

"It's behind the home team sideline," said Bob. "There's a three-quarter cement barrier painted crimson red around it. Just flip the metal cover back and hit the all the switches and turn on the spigot."

"And the lights?" asked Monroe.

"In the press box," replied Bob. "You'll need the key to open it. Head upstairs; the first door you see on the left, open it. The box is on the wall to the right. It's got a red apple sticker on it; you can't miss it. And be sure to turn them all on." Bob struggled to reach his key ring, a collection of at least two-dozen.

"For Christ sake, do you have a key to every home in Red Orchard?" joked Monroe. Bob rummaged through all the keys before sliding the appropriate key off the key chain.

"Everyone ready?" asked the sheriff.

"I'm not a real religious person," said Paula, "but I think we should maybe say a prayer and hope God's on our side tonight."

"Amen to that," added Monroe.

The four adults grasped their hands together. "God, if you're up there, give us the strength to win this battle and restore normalcy to our city."

"Not bad, young lady," said Bob. "Okay guys, let's take care of business."

Chapter 11

The three stormed out of the car. Paula sprinted like a track-and-field star to midfield. She felt terrified yet exhilarated at the same time – a strange mixture for sure. She reached into her pocket and pulled out the taped-up clothespins, two managing to nip her fingers.

"Ow, you little piss heads!" Paula pried them off her now bleeding fingers and hung up the red towel. For good measure, she wiped the blood along the wire. "Come and get it!"

Monroe huffed and puffed his way up the stairs. He swore if he made it through this horrific night, he'd lose a few pounds and get in keen physical shape.

The deputy unlocked the door at the top of the stairs and pulled the string dangling there front and center in the room. The dimly lit light bulb barely provided enough light. He turned, searching around the wall for the apple sticker.

"Ah, there you are." The deputy inserted the yellow-coated key and turned it, opening the electrical box. There, he saw three rows of switches, twelve in all. "All righty, here it goes."

The stadium lights emitted a faint glow, like an early morning dawn. The deputy expected them to turn on right away like any desk lamp. Instead, they brightened at a snail's pace. He went over to the microphone, tapping it. "This thing on? Testing one, two, three." He could hear his voice echoing all over the premises. "All right folks, let's get this show on the road and kick some clippie ass!"

***

Paula glanced up, smirking, as she raced back to the truck, feeling better now that the whole field would soon be on full display. She closed the back door and patted Bob on the shoulder. "We're almost there." He didn't respond. "Hey, Bob, you alright?" Paula clutched the headrest and pulled herself forward. His eyes were closed, mouth slightly agape.

Paula spotted movement from under his jacket, then a sound like kids churning their little hands in mud. Paula tugged him on the shoulder. Still no response. "Oh God, no."

From the top of Bob's jacket, a clippie emerged with bloodstains around its mouth. She jumped outside the truck on her hands and knees, almost throwing up. She tried to scream, but couldn't.

The sheriff dashed over to the sprinklers. He knelt down, lightheaded. Following Bob's instructions, he pressed multiple blue buttons then turned the rusted spigot handles all the way clockwise. Monroe came down the stairs. "We're all good upstairs" said Monroe. "You okay?"

"I think so," answered Taylor. "Paula should be back at the truck by now. Now all we need is Bob to do his thing and hope for the best."

***

Paula trembled, but regained her composure, finally yelling out to her co-workers.

"Sounds like she's in trouble!" said Monroe.

The two rushed back only to find Paula in tears. Through the window, they saw Bob's lifeless body sitting in the driver's side. Taylor opened the driver's side door, spotting blood all over Bob's lap and the interior seat. Both he and the deputy saw movement under the jacket.

Monroe put on a brave face as he stretched out his arm and reached for the metal zipper. The deputy narrowed his eyes, pulling it down. There, a half-dozen clippies feasted on Bob's midsection.

"Oh shit, they're still eating him!" Monroe turned Wonder Bread white in shock. He quickly zipped it back up and stumbled out of the truck, landing on his ass.

"Goddamn it," muttered Taylor. He rubbed the bridge of his nose with his thumb and index finger. There was no time to weep. They needed a plan ASAP or they'd all be dead too. Then he spoke under his breath. "Bait."

"Bait? Did you just say bait?" asked Paula, horrified." What the hell are you talking about?"

"I don't want to sound cold-hearted, but we need to use him to attract the other clippies. I've got a whole damn town to save and I don't think we can rely on a ratty old towel to do the trick."

Paula and Monroe looked at each other. They were fresh out of ideas. "What do you need us to do?" asked Monroe.

The two men of the law grabbed Bob's body from the truck and struggled to carry him to where the red towel was pinned. Hundreds, maybe thousands of clippies hovered above. They set Bob down and made a sign of the cross in deep gratitude for everything he had done.

The sprinkler system finally ticked on, sputtering into high gear. The two men got soaked as they darted back to the truck. Paula was still shaken up, staring out at the football field. She'd never seen a dead person before, only in the movies. In a matter of seconds, a swarm of clippies zeroed in on the lifeless body.

"There!" pointed Monroe as more descended onto the long stretch of wire. The well-lit field soon turned into a sea of darkness as thousands of clippies began perching themselves along the metal clothesline, throbbing and glowing like a string of Christmas lights.

Monroe pulled out his phone. "Who are you calling?" asked Taylor.

"The Baldwins," replied Monroe. "I want to know if any clippies are still there." Mr. Baldwin answered the phone. They spoke briefly before Monroe then hung up.

"Good news guys," smiled Monroe, relieved. "Apparently there are no clippies up at their house, or at their neighbors. Let's hope we got 'em all here." The three peered out at the field. Every inch of space of wire seemed to be filled with clippies. Monroe thought of Alfred Hitchcock's *The Birds*.

"So how do we do this?" asked Paula. "Bob never told us what to do?"

"We'll figure it out," said Taylor. "First of all, we start the truck."

The sheriff reached over and turned the keys. The big eight-cylinder engine rumbled. Taylor quietly opened the door and slipped on a pair of work gloves he found in the back seat. He rounded the front of the truck and picked up the jumper cables.

Taylor climbed up the truck bed and clipped one end of the cables to the outstretched wire. Holding the other end, he stepped down and shifted over to the battery. He inched closer, but the cable was too short.

"Damn it, we're too far away!"

"I got it!" shouted Monroe, trying to be heard over the rumbling engine. He jumped into the blood-stained driver's seat and backed up the truck. "Are we set?"

"Another couple of feet and we're good!" Taylor called out.

A wave of clippies descended from out of the sky and pounced on Taylor like strafing hawks. He dropped the cables as the wooden objects gnashed and gnawed on his exposed flesh.

Monroe hurried out of the truck and swatted the clippies off the sheriff. "Take the cable!" screamed Taylor, covering up in a protective ball. The deputy hesitated. "Just do it!"

The deputy picked up the cable with his bare hands and touched the battery connection. From end zone to end zone came a bright flash of light trailed the line of wire. Monroe stumbled backwards and accidently touched both red and black ends. He felt a tremendous jolt as he fell to the ground, shaking. Paula jumped out and rushed over to him.

The deputy wasn't moving. She started giving him CPR. "Come on you!" She pressed her palms against his chest repeatedly, stopping when the deputy started coughing.

Monroe opened his eyes halfway and whispered, signaling Paula to move closer to his face. "Need more . . . mouth to mouth." Paula gave him a big hug then helped him off the ground.

The sheriff, wounded and exhausted as all hell, emerged from a lifeless pile of clippies. As Paula helped him to his feet, the three peered at the outstretched wire and noticed the glowing clippies abruptly shorting out. They dropped from the wire, and from the sky like hail, falling harmlessly onto the turf.

"Did we win?" asked the dazed deputy, still trying to regain his bearings, his hair singed and disheveled as he leaned up against the truck for a moment. They caught their collective breathe then cautiously approached midfield, staring at all the clothespins littering the football field. Under a large mound was Cortland's body, completely buried underneath.

"They're all dead?" asked Paula.

"As dead as clothespins can get, I reckon," said Monroe.

"We'll need to scour the town for any more of these little buggers," added the sheriff, suggesting making another all-points bulletin on the radio. "Paula, bring the truck around; Deputy, help me with Mr. Cortland's body."

Chapter 15

Six months later and twenty-five pounds lighter, newly anointed Sheriff Thomas Monroe had returned to work, sunburned and rested from a week vacation in the Florida Keys with his girlfriend Paula, now a full-time reporter for the local *Red Orchard Times* newspaper. She still maintained her part-time gig at the police station. Former Sheriff Mike Taylor, freshly retired and fully recovered from his wounds, became a consultant for a home security company in nearby Macoun County.

Monroe quickly developed a reputation for being dedicated and detailed. He was working late and, as usual, alone, following up on some paperwork, the worst part of the job. Now he understood why his former boss was cranky at times, especially on a Friday evening – he didn't get paid overtime.

The sheriff put down his pen and took a break, his right hand cramping up again. He walked over to the front door, admiring his newly svelte frame in the reflection. No more donuts, he promised himself. Normally he'd be snacking on cookies and soda, but now it was strictly raw veggies, fruits, and bottled water. He could fully relate to his co-worker Holly's dieting hell, but he felt good.

Ping. Ping. Ping. There was that sound again, like someone tapping their knuckles on a dense slab of wood. Paula had mentioned it before; Holly too. It seemed to come and go. The sheriff wandered into the seldom-used office, the official storage facility of the Red Orchard Police Department. Monroe listened intently. He knelt down, trying to pinpoint the direction.

He narrowed the sound to the storage room. He opened the door and followed it to the deep corner. He pushed some boxes aside and saw the safe, slightly bigger than a standard college dorm room refrigerator. The sound abruptly stopped. Perplexed, he pulled out his set of keys and selected the particularly odd-shaped one. He placed it in the slot and turned. Just as he opened the door, he vaguely remembered something. The shock he received from the live wire had deleted a few memory details.

He peered deep into the safe. It was mainly used to store outdated evidence, a relic from the 1930's. But in a town as safe as Red Orchard, it was basically an antique gathering dust. Inside was the original deed to the building and a vintage revolver discovered during the renovation project when it was converted from the old post office into the current police station.

There was a rustling sound under the papers in the back. Monroe couldn't see anything but thought maybe it was a cockroach. He hated cockroaches. Suddenly his fuzzy memory started to come into focus. A chill rose up his scoliosis-free spine. "No way."

Before he could close the door, a pair of clippies shot out like bullets. The sheriff fell over backwards, stunned. Fearing they might escape, he scuttled to the door, slamming it shut. He pulled out his gun and huffed. "All right you clippie bastards, show yourselves!"

One swooped down, latching onto the back of the sheriff's neck, sampling a tasty morsel of Monroe's flesh. "Ouch! Damn you!" He reached around, but it vanished.

Monroe started sweating. He wiped the perspiration from his eyes when he heard a click. The lights went out. Monroe shifted over and extended his arm to turn on the light switch back on when he felt a familiar sensation. The two clippies ambushed the sheriff's hand, nipping and gnawing at his fingers, drawing blood.

Monroe tried to flick on the lights with his elbow, but the switch handle was snapped off.

"You little shits!" He could hear the clippies buzzing around the room like evil bees. He reached for his cell phone and shined the light frantically around the dark room. Nothing.

The sheriff backed up against the door when he spotted the two clippies perched on top of the five-drawer metal file cabinet. They creaked their vicious little wooden mouths, opening and closing in slow motion like breathing goldfish. Monroe held his phone steady, directing the light at the clothespins. He raised his gun and aimed, about to reel off a shot when they darted away.

"Damn it." The sheriff scanned the room. He stood silent for what seemed like hours. Suddenly, he noticed debris floating down from the ceiling like snowflakes.

He spotted them, trying to burrow through the water stained ceiling tiles. Monroe raised his gun and fired, no hesitation this time. Pop-Pop-Pop. He shifted his body, not wanting to catch a ricochet in the face.

The dust settled. Monroe, still crouched on the floor, heard a faint scratching sound. He stood up and slowly panned the light around his feet. There, lying on the unkempt checkered linoleum floor were the clippies. One of them was blown away in half, non-responsive. The other was partially wounded. The sheriff watched it struggle along the floor, the twisted metal spring barely holding the two slivers of wood together.

Monroe bent down on one knee and gazed at the ordinary wooden clothespin. He pointed the gun barrel almost point blank but suddenly paused. For a second he felt . . . To hell with that. Monroe blasted the hell out of the inanimate object, blowing it to pieces.

Paula suddenly burst through the door, scared out of her wits. "What the hell is going on? Honey, are you okay?"

The small room was filled with dust and gun smoke. Monroe waved it aside and hugged Paula. "God, I really, really hate clothespins."

The Road Taken

Christopher Wolfe, age forty-six, was traveling late on the Florida Turnpike, his destination South Bay, a small, sweaty town that butted up against the Everglades. He was returning from a job interview up in Marietta, Georgia. Things were looking bleak for the former county IT specialist, out of work for months, now doing mostly freelance work to pay the bills. He'd been scouring job sites ever since the Clewiston County commissioners decided to Ginzue the town budget.

Wolfe drove up the night before to prep for the early Monday morning interview. He slept in a twenty-nine dollar a night fleabag motel, doing his best to conserve every dollar he had for gas, food, and tolls. The next day, Wolfe awoke to the harmonious sounds of screeching police sirens. He felt achy after sleeping on a mattress so old and broken in that Union Army General, William Tecumseh Sherman, had probably caught twenty winks on it before his infamous march to the sea. Still, Wolfe managed to catch an energetic boost after a non-heated shower. He dined on a pair of Strawberry-frosted Pop Tarts then guzzled down a twenty-ounce bottle of Tropicana orange juice chilling in his cooler.

Wolfe arrived fifteen minutes prior to the interview. After a slight delay, he strolled into the conference room, where three people greeted him.

The interrogation went well. Two of the three interviewers were fair and professional, while the other treated the experience like the dentist scene from the film *Marathon Man* – the only thing missing was the drill. Wolfe laid on the schmooze and smarts. The two women were impressed. The lone man, tall and skinny as a totem pole, preferred to dissect his employment history with a sharpened scalpel. Still, Wolfe handled the grilling well. He walked out feeling unscathed and optimistic.

"We'll contact you by the end of the week," said the plump middle-aged woman with a wink, her dyed locks hued in Bozo the Clown orange. Wolfe had heard that phrase a few times too many. Always close, but not close enough. Still . . .

On the trip home, Wolfe was making good time until he got bogged down in commuter traffic outside of Macon. Stuck in the blistering mid-August sun, he could only watch in dismay as the temperature gauge on the dashboard pinned red. In seconds, the front grill began boiling over like a geyser.

After giving the car ample time to simmer down on the side of the road, he refilled the drained radiator halfway with the melted ice from his red plastic cooler. It was enough to get him to a Flying J where he topped it off with more water. He hurried in real quick and bought a package of Nutter Butters for the tedious journey.

As Wolfe approached his car, he noticed drips of oil emanating from between the two front tires, which were showing a receding tread line. He rifled off a string of expletives before plopping down in the driver's seat. *More car repairs; that's all I need right now!* He slumped his head onto the steering wheel in defeat. Then he sat back up and took a glance of himself in the rearview mirror and sighed. *I've got to land this job.*

He sighed before sputtering out of the gas station parking lot. At least the transmission on his faded yellow 1989 Volvo wagon was ox-strong, still hanging in there despite a quarter of a million miles. Lately, Wolfe patted the steering wheel every time it started up.

After a few hours of problem-free driving, he swung by a Wendy's for dinner and hit the drive-thru. He got back on the turnpike minutes later and set the cruise control at sixty-five-miles an hour as he chowed down on a Baconator with medium French fries and a large Coke. He felt good, savoring the triple decker burger with every bite. *Oh man, I needed that,* Wolfe thought, belching so loud it made his innards vibrate. Feeling relieved yet tired, he glanced at his watch and thought, *It's almost one in the morning, for God's sake. I've got another two hours to go!*

Indigestion reared its ugly head. He munched on a couple of fruit-flavored Tums and continued home.

Up ahead, he noticed a trail of breaking red lights. The traffic began backing up quickly. *Now what?* He turned on the radio and shifted the knob, trying to pinpoint a traffic update. "Oh, swell," grimaced Wolfe. A tractor-trailer loaded with poultry had jackknifed, snarling up the two-lane stretch of highway for what could be hours.

This is really going to put me in a fowl mood, he thought. Wolfe despised traffic jams of any sort, becoming claustrophobic in a heartbeat. He certainly couldn't afford to let his Volvo lose its cool again. He had to at least keep moving – like a shark.

Wolfe started pressing. He glanced at the temperature gauge which was inching past the halfway mark. *I can't deal with this crap again!*

Wolfe skirted off the next exit a mile ahead, three-quarters convinced there was a way to circumvent the roadside mess.

The rural road ran parallel to the railroad tracks, a sure sign he was in the heart of Podunk country. He popped open his last Coke from the cooler, still brisk despite being void of ice for some time. His eyelids began a slow droop.

"No, no, no, Mr. Wolfe." He gave himself a quick slap on the cheeks. Wolfe yawned then rolled down the window. The warm breeze gave him a mild wake up call. Cranking the Buzzcocks provided more relief.

"I don't know what to do with my life!" howled Wolfe, singing along to one of his favorite tunes. He slumped his shoulders. *How apropos.* He was on the wrong side of forty and technically middle aged., unemployed, and drifting.

The desolate stretch of road abruptly turned into a meandering snake as he approached State Road 78, hugging Lake Okeechobee. There were a lot of nonfunctioning roadside light poles along the side of the road. The rural darkness felt uneasy. Maybe he should have stuck to the highway. Probably. For certain.

He began observing the dilapidated houses on each side of the road, set back too far to really matter. Just as he pried a Doors CD from its jewel case, something darted across the worn asphalt. The front passenger tire blew out. The car swerved violently. Wolfe applied the brakes carefully, remembering not to slam them. The car spiraled off the side of the road into a field of tall grass before coming to a complete halt.

"Dammit," he said, unbuckling the seatbelt. The putrid stench of burnt rubber flowed into the car, making Wolfe gag. He stepped outside and shook his head, exasperated with his hands on his hips. Wolfe paused for a moment before noticing a low rolling fog creeping over the palmetto scrub on both sides of the road. *This is not good*, he thought.

Wolfe reached back into the car for the rechargeable flashlight he stored in the glove compartment. He grabbed it, handling it like a squirt gun before revving the handle over and over. He cursed the meager beam of light, thinking he should have coughed up a few bucks for something halfway decent. But beggars can't be choosy; it had been a free gift from his long-time State Farm insurance agent.

He rounded the front of the car and knelt down to inspect the damage. *Holy shit.* The tire was complete history, shredded like a Freddy Kruger victim. A deep, curving gash encompassed half of the low budget Goodyear radial. *What the hell?*

Wolfe used to help out at his dad's car repair shop, mostly during the summer months to earn money to pay for an occasional college class or case of beer. He'd seen his fair share of flat tires before, but never anything like this.

An echoing howl seeped over from the encroaching embankment, the shape hidden by the scrub landscape. Wolfe peered over, revving the flashlight again and again. *Piece of crap.* The five-minute charge wasn't cutting it.

He darted over and opened the tailgate, scrambling to uncover the third row seat. He pulled out the spare, smooth as dolphin skin, and prepped the jack.

The sound grew louder. Whatever it was, it was moving closer. Wolfe stood up and scouted the harsh, central Florida terrain. He was wide awake now.

One by one he removed the lug nuts. The last one wouldn't budge. "Son of a bitch!" Wolfe placed his foot on the plus-shaped lug wrench and applied all his weight, finally turning it loose. He quickly mounted the tire, tightening each lug nut with his fingers first before finishing up with the lug wrench. He gathered up the tools and headed back to the tailgate.

The sound had gotten even closer. Wolfe revved the bright yellow flashlight again. A whip of a tail flashed near the driver's side of the car, snapping off the side view mirror. Fearful, Wolfe crouched down near the rear wheel well. Breathing heavily, Wolfe decided to roll the flat tire past the front of the car, hoping to distract whatever was beginning to scare the hell out of him.

The thing screeched. A greenish limb with elongated claws abruptly attacked the blown tire, further mincing it to pieces.

Wolfe grasped the lug nut wrench in his right hand and jumped inside the car and slammed the tailgate. He started to climb over the middle row seat when the car started tipping back and forth. Wolfe dove for the front of the car and laid on the horn. The thing suddenly hurdled up onto the roof, digging its claws deep into the metal. Wolfe looked up, horrified as the five-inch nails cut through the top like aluminum foil.

Wolfe laid on the horn again then accidently turned on the wipers. The thing retracted its claws and lunged at the windshield. The ragged-toothed mouth snapped wildly as it ripped off the wiper blades, leaving a trail of cascading saliva on the glass.

"Help me!" shouted Wolfe as he bounced around inside the car like a pinball. Wolfe knew a little something about Florida wildlife, but this was something totally messed up. It appeared to be a bizarre concoction of kangaroo and crocodile, with just a hint of Gila monster thrown in for good measure. Whatever it was, it was weird and pissed off. And now it was tearing his beloved Volvo apart.

Wolfe frantically searched for his keys but couldn't find them. The creature impaled the aftermarket plastic sunroof with its claws and pried it off like a Tupperware lid. The creature dipped its lizard-long muscular neck inside and began thrashing its jaws about. Wolfe eyed a can of WD-40 that had rolled out from under the front passenger seat. He grabbed it, flicking the narrow red stem and fired away into its eyes and mouth. The creature gagged and squealed, retreating momentarily.

Terrified, Wolfe quickly stuck his head out of the sunroof and screamed until his lungs and throat burned.

He heard a gunshot and ducked back inside the car. *Oh crap . . . now what!*

Wolfe heard more gunshots ring out from the tall scrub. One of bullets took out the rear driver's side taillight. He revved the flashlight again but couldn't see anything. Suddenly, the creature bulldozed into the passenger side door, cracking the glass. Wolfe yelled out – more shots echoed from the woods. The creature leaped onto the roof of the car again, this time letting out a menacing roar. The creature stuck its deep forest green frame partially through the opening. The creature's ivory teeth were all lined up like a picket fence, eager to rip Wolfe to pieces. He gave the creature a double dose of lug wrench and WD-40, but it kept on attacking.

Wolfe's back seared with pain, pressing uncomfortably against the hard-steering wheel, the horn wailing nonstop. He screamed out again and again until he couldn't utter a syllable. He managed to shift the driver's seat back, allowing him to get more leverage as he fended off the creature with multiple kicks to the head.

More shots rang out, sounding more powerful . . . and closer than before. One whizzed straight though the car door, narrowly missing Wolfe's head.

"Aaagh!"

The creature had gotten a hold of his right foot when it abruptly slumped over. The head and elongated neck dangled inside the car, motionless. Wolfe gagged as blood and drool ran down its mouth, falling smackdab into Wolfe's lap. He pried his worn black dress shoe from the dead creature's ragged jaw, snagged on one of its front teeth. He made an undignified roll out of the driver's side door and spilled out into a patch of low damp grass. The moist ground cooled his banged-up perspiring body. Wolfe dug deep to fill his lungs with air before nearly passing out.

He heard rustling in the tall grass almost upon him.

"Are you okay, sir?" said an authoritative voice.

Wolfe twitched in fright. He slowly opened his eyes, a bright light now forcing him to squint. "Who are you — what are you?" he asked in a hoarse voice.

A group of five men stood over him. Two of them helped him up, shifting away from the car. The other three men strapped on rubber gloves and started examining the dead creature.

Wolfe limped towards the street as he rubbed his eyes and creaked his back. "Are you with Florida Fish and Game?" He then focused on their camouflaged uniforms. "Oh shit, you guys are military?"

"A little bit of both," replied one of the men, rather abruptly. He handed Wolfe a towel to clean himself off. "And you, sir?"

"Uh, unemployed IT specialist returning from a job interview."

"I didn't know you guys interviewed at night," said one of the men inspecting the dead creature with the end of his weapon. "What dedication."

"We're a unique breed," answered Wolfe, coughing. His frazzled body ached all over. "Actually, the interview was up in Georgia earlier today. I was just returning home — cross your fingers because I really need a job."

Wolf finished cleaning up and attempted to hand the towel back to the man.

"No thanks," said the man, chewing on a big wad of bubble gum.

Wolfe glanced over to the three men removing the creature. "What the hell is that . . . thing?"

"New species discovered in the Everglades," replied another man, guzzling water from a black metal bottle.

"The Everglades?" replied Wolfe. "Since when did the everglades turn into *Jurassic Park*?"

The man standing next to him, wearing a black baseball cap backwards, laughed. *"Jurassic Park. Funny."*

"You have no idea what's brewing out here," said the man chewing gum.

"There aren't more of them out there?" Wolfe glanced back as three of the men finished removing the carcass from his squashed-up Volvo.

"What you got is a bunch of idiots disposing their exotic pets into the Glades," said the one wearing the cap. "It's becoming a freak show of nature out there, and we're here to monitor it."

The man chewing gum chimed in. "You heard of frankenfish?"

"Uh, vaguely," answered Wolfe.

"Well, that whacked out combo is really a cross between a piranha and largemouth bass. Crazy shit out here, my friend."

"That makes perfect sense," replied Wolfe, "But that still doesn't explain crocaroo here" chided Wolfe as he pointed at the deceased creature, now nice and snug in a black nylon body bag.

The man in the cap giggled as he watched the three men finishing zipping up the bag. "Croc-a-roo; this guy is good."

"Zip it," barked the man in charge, now blowing a bubble.

Wolfe stumbled over to his Swedish delight and leaned against it. "My poor car; it's totaled. What am I gonna do?"

The man in charge eyed Wolfe. "You got your resume handy?"

"What?" barked Wolfe, exasperated that his life (like his car) seemed totally ruined. He reached into the back seat and pulled out a blue folder from his briefcase and took a copy. He presented it to him.

The man in charge scanned the one-page document top to bottom. "Your qualifications look pretty solid, and we could sure use a new IT guy ASAP."

"Really?" said Wolfe. "That would be great. Um, if you don't mind me asking, what happened to the last one?"

All five men looked at each without uttering a word before the man donning the cap spoke up.

"He got a transfer."

"Uh, yeah," said the leader, clearing his throat. "Tell you what, Mr. Wolfe. If you don't get that gig up in Georgia, we'd like you to work for us. We can start you off at, say, 85K."

"Hell, after what happened to your car, we'll even throw in a company Jeep," added the gum chewer. Wolfe's eyes lit up. Eighty-five grand would come in handy right about now. And a car to boot!

"Anything else I need to know before I sign on the dotted line?" inquired Wolfe, forgetting about his interview in Georgia altogether.

"First off, you'll be working with 'former' military people and top scientists, dedicated professionals just like yourself," said the leader. "You'll run the computers, provide statistics every month, learn to handle a firearm – just in case . . . Oh, and if I'm not mistaken, our health benefits are pretty kick ass."

"Sounds great . . . I'm sorry," stammered Wolfe, "In case of what?"

The man chewing gum turned to Wolfe. "More croc-a-roos."

I Saw It Coming

"Is it all right if I try to explain, you know – before we . . .?" asked the lean unkempt man. He resembled an aging rock star with his long bleached-out hair and weathered skin, tan and wrinkled.

Sitting across from him was a young detective. He was a shade over six feet tall, smartly dressed in a charcoal gray suit and sporting a properly trimmed mustache and wire rimmed glasses. The two sat alone in a room, used primarily for interrogations.

"That's why I'm in this room. I want to hear your side of the story."

"Thank you, sir," the man replied.

"Well, where would you like to start?" asked the detective.

The homeless man had been arrested for the murders of six people. A veteran cop handling the case said it was a slam dunk. No if, ands, or buts. The detective was told the man did have a record, arrested for minor offences, public intoxication, etc. That didn't sound like a mass murderer to him.

The detective's stomach grumbled, reverberating like a pack of howling coyotes. He'd missed breakfast and it was nearing one in the afternoon. Still, he was told the guy's tale was a real doozy. The man nodded in appreciation, rubbing his handcuffed hands on his face and pausing to take in a deep breath.

"Don't leave anything out; I want to hear all the details," said the detective.

The man narrowed his eyes, not sure if he was being played with.

"I saw it coming. I saw it coming a mile away," he began. "No one else seemed interested or concerned, but I was. I saw it coming, clear as day."

"And where were you again?" the detective asked, partially familiar with the case.

"I was at Gato Beach, as always. It's a nice secluded parcel of sand off the beaten path. It's kinda like my own little sanctuary. Not many people go there."

"Gato Beach?" asked the detective.

"Oh, I call it Gato Beach because so many stray cats like to hang out there. *Gato* means 'cat' in Spanish. I feed 'em when I can afford it.

"That's nice. Continue," instructed the detective.

"Well, it was late Sunday afternoon, still warm and humid out. I was by myself, as always. The best place in the whole wide world for a homeless man is the beach, you know why?"

"Why is that?"

"You got showers, the sun, and of course, the Gulf of Mexico. I feel normal there – like anyone else, just soaking up the rays and enjoying a swim here and there. I pick up food money by making hats from palm leaves. I'm pretty good at it."

"I'm sure you are."

"After what I saw, I swore to myself I would never ever set foot on that beach again so help me God. It's why I was planning to move on from here, getting a job and such. I wasn't planning no getaway like that cop thought. I just wanted fresh start, if I could." With a wilted smile, the man held up the cuffs secured to his slender wrists.

'Yeah, that may not be happening," sighed the detective. The homeless man was the lone suspect in the grisly deaths. "But if you could?"

"I was thinking of moving to my home state of Kentucky or maybe North Carolina. Got a brother there. I could get back into teaching again or camp counseling. You know, I used to teach at a middle school back in Louisville."

"Really? I bet you'd miss the sea and sand," said the detective.

"Yeah, no ocean there, only the Ohio River, and I'm sure as heck not gonna go for a swim in that water. Some parts are so thick with pollution the fish haft'a learn to walk." He cracked himself up. The detective let out a chuckle.

"Always liked that joke," said the homeless man. "But seriously, mister, I didn't kill nobody. My story is gonna stay the same no matter who I tell. And when it's the truth you're telling, it's easy to remember; you know what I mean?"

"If you don't mind me asking, what made you move to the Sunshine State?"

The man sighed. "I guess it's a place where people like me end up I suppose – those who messed up a bunch in life. It's the last stop on the map for a lot of folks. For me, it's been a stopgap from reality, or maybe just an extended vacation. Either way, I thank God for the sun and surf of Florida."

The detective smirked. "A sunny place for shady people. Continue."

"Well, I was lying on my back, arms folded out, hands behind my head, and chilling on my trusty orange-striped beach towel. Sometimes I'll sit up with my legs crisscross apple sauce just surveying the landscape."

"Crisscross apple sauce?"

"It's an expression we teachers use when workin' with children. You have any children?"

"I have a son. He's two, but so far no crisscross apple sauce."

"He'll learn," replied the homeless man with a smile. "Maybe he'll grow up to be a detective like his old man."

The detective smiled. "Maybe."

"So there I was, peering out into the water. The color of the Gulf always looks better through sunglasses, did you ever notice that? It's like turquoise. Just beautiful."

The homeless man shifted in his chair, his shackled arms in his lap. "This strange object seemed to target the half-dozen folks still enjoying the rest of the setting sun. Whatever it was, it was headed straight for the beach, no question about it, like some evil torpedo. I didn't see much at first. No dorsal fin sticking up high like a sail, but the movement was there. It cut through the water with a lot of force, against the grain of the current."

"And?"

"I stood up and took off my sunglasses just to make sure. Maybe I don't look like the most trustworthy type. I know my outwardly appearance looks rather disheveled."

"Nice word – disheveled, that is."

"Thanks. I know a few," the man replied. "Like I said, I used to be a teacher. I still got some of that country twang in me, though. Some people automatically think..."

"No harm in that," replied the detective, originally from neighboring Ohio."

"No harm at all, sir." The man paused again, then continued. "Well, I was wearing my customary Levi cut-offs, nothing fancy, unlike those stupid bathing suits guys wear today that trail past your knees. What's the point of wearing something so long at the beach? How are you supposed to get a decent suntan? They make you look like a little man, a midget – I guess that's not politically correct to say today, but that's what they look like to me."

The detective leaned back, still crossing his arms. "Can you get to the point?"

"I'm getting there." The man gave the detective an icy stare before getting back to his yarn.

"I stood up, making sure I was seeing something and not a mirage. I walked down to the water's edge, the waves pushing gently just over my ankles. It felt good and warm – the Gulf of Mexico's like that, not like the cold Atlantic. Well, it was harder to see at water level, so I trudged back up the hill to where the dunes are. You see lizards and stuff up there all the time – an occasional beer can or a fast food bag, but I clean those up, pronto.

"I'm sure you do," said the detective.

"What you really gotta watch out for them bastard sand spurs. You step on one of those mothers and you're in for a world of hurt."

"I'm familiar with them," said the detective. He glanced at this watch and gestured with his hand for the man to pick up the pace.

"Sorry. From up there I could see it coming, clear as a bell. It was maybe thirty yards from shore now, paddling hard. It looked real dark in the clear water. And long, big as a Cadillac. It wasn't too wide though – maybe like one of those silly little smart cars – those are just plain stupid, aren't they? I like big cars that get shitty gas mileage. Sorry for the curse word.

"It happens." The detective perked up a bit, his hands placed on his thighs as the homeless man appeared to be getting to the meaty part of the story. "Go on."

"Anyway, I started hollering for everyone to get out of the water and off the beach. I swear I tried. I come running down the dune, even stepped on a bunch of sand spurs, but I didn't care. I yanked 'em all out in a split second. I was too worried about those people. I swear to God."

"What did they do?" the detective asked, inching up in his chair, his eyes getting bigger.

"They just stood there like statues. I may not look like Ivy League material, but I certainly know monsters when I see 'em. And this thing was gaining speed. If people didn't leave that beach it was gonna be a blood bath. I went up to this couple – they had two beautiful children. They were building cute little sandcastles, paying no mind. Everybody thought I was crazy, even though it was getting closer – the outline of the body, like that submarine from *Twenty Thousand Leagues Under the Sea.* What was the name?"

"The Nautilus," said the detective as he loosened his tie and undid the top button. "So, no one paid any attention to you?"

"Not one," answered the man. "I screamed, pleading my guts out. That's when they started cursing at me, trying to shush me like I was in some goddamn library. This one guy with his perfect hair and designer shirt with the gator on it came over and grabbed my arm – tells me to get the hell away, or else."

"And?"

"I didn't want to die, so I left. I know when I'm not wanted, trust me. It happens a lot to people like us."

"What did you do next?"

"I hurried back up that dune, away from the beach and hid behind one of the royal palms – they're majestic."

"And then what?"

"I hope you don't think I'm wasting your time, but this is important, and it's the God's honest truth."

"Not at all, please continue," the detective replied. He didn't believe the validity of the man's story (how could he?), but either way, he was totally hooked.

"It was almost at the shore. I hollered one last time, cupping my mouth with my hands. That's when that guy with the gator shirt took notice. He saw it coming, but by then it was too late. He had it coming all right, for being so damn pigheaded. It's just a shame, a goddamn shame."

The perspiring detective stood up and took off his jacket, hanging it on the chair. He sat down, rolled up his sleeves, and wiped his brow. "So, they just stood there and did nothing?"

"Yep." The man started tearing up. "The screaming and the blood, that's all I remember. I crouched down so hard, hiding behind the scrub and sea oats. I didn't want to look . . . but I had to."

"Like a car wreck," surmised the detective.

"I was petrified like a stone. I felt like burying myself in the sand to hide."

"And this thing attacked all the people on the beach?"

"It ambushed them, storming out from the shallow waters with its flipper legs and huge jaw filled with teeth. They were bright white, blinding as porcelain. And long. No one had a chance."

"Was it a crocodile?" asked the detective. "Because there are crocodiles in Florida."

"Nah," replied the man. "This thing looked was bigger. It kinda looked like one of those prehistoric sea creatures. The eyes. I remember the eyes, big as a softball . . . Oh my God."

"It's okay."

"Not for those people, it wasn't," snapped the man. "Those dumb grownups, their innocent children – all slaughtered. That thing just tore them to pieces...just tore them to pieces. I'm sorry – it's just that..." The man started weeping.

"You need a tissue?"

"No, I'm all right." The man sniffled and wiped his nose with his arm sleeve. The man regained his composure, his tone changing to indignation. "This didn't need to happen, detective. I warned them, all of them, what was gonna happen, but they didn't believe me. Aren't you supposed to listen to someone warning you? You should respect that!"

The detective nodded in agreement.

"I'm not dumb, you know. I graduated from college, had a good job. Why are people like this?"

"Judgmental is the word," said the detective.

People don't listen and they end up paying the price. People really need to listen more, you know what I mean? Why is that so difficult?"

"Listening is a lost art, like thinking, I suppose," said the detective.

The homeless man nodded. He squinted, noticing beads of sweat on the detective's forehead. "Are you okay, sir? You seem a bit anxious."

"I'm fine," the detective replied. "Just a bit warm in here."

"It's all true, sir, so help me God. You *do* believe me…don't you?"

The detective exhaled. He took off his glasses and rubbed the bridge of his nose. There was a knock at the door.

The homeless man looked up and noticed two police officers through the square window. "I guess it's time to go?"

The detective stood up as he waved the two officers to enter the room. "I guess so."

"Well, why the hell not," the man said. "Since no one believes me. Just like at the beach."

As the homeless man was escorted away, he glanced back at the detective. "By the way, detective, you're looking a bit disheveled yourself."

The detective nodded as he watched the man being led away.

***

Weeks later, a young couple jogging in the early morning near the same pristine white sand beach stumbled across body parts along the shoreline, a hand and tattered arm with a faded slate blue tattoo. After a detailed investigation, the victims turned out to a pair of missing retirement-aged fishermen. Also noted along the bloodstained beach were strange flipper-like imprints just like the ones the homeless man had previously described to a tee. A diligent police officer also discovered a four-inch tooth fragment.

The following week, the groomed homeless man, clean shaven and presentable, was released, no questions asked. After spending some time at a cheap motel, the tab paid in full courtesy of the local police department, he returned to the scene of the crime. The man sported a fresh pair of knee-length khaki shorts that he rolled up and a light blue tee shirt. He picked up a forgotten pink-and-yellow beach chair resting against the water fountain then marched up the sand dune and planted it between the towering royal palm trees.

He sat down and took in a deep, salt-aired breath. The Gulf was flat, barely a ripple registering on the bath warm water. A gentleman sporting an orange golf shirt and blue jeans approached the beach and called out to the man.

"So, this is paradise, huh?" The detective scaled up the sandy dune and handed the homeless man a chilled Presidente beer. The two clanked bottles and took synchronized gulps. A pair of dying palm fronds rattled above in the breeze.

"So, this is your way of apologizing?"

"The tip of the iceberg, Mr. Olsen" said the detective.

"Bud is fine, Mr. Detective, but it's gonna take a hell of a lot more than a single beer."

"I wholeheartedly agree, Bud." The detective took another sip and added. "By the way, it's Jensen, Lee Jensen." He extended his arm and the two shook hands. "I heard you got yourself a nice settlement."

"Yeah, wrongful arrest and such," said Bud. "My lawyer said he might put my face on one of his giant billboard ads you see on Interstate 75."

There was an awkward moment of silence when the detective spoke up.

"You know it was a difficult case for us," said Jensen. "I mean, none of us at the station believed a sea monster could be . . ."

"I understand," said Bud. "Blaming anything on a sea monster would sound stupid, and I don't fault you folks slapping the cuffs on me."

"So, what are you going to do now?" asked Jensen.

"Well, there's still time to get my life in order."

"I'd say so," replied Jensen, adding that he had a cooler full of beers and a pizza back in his car.

"Twist my arm," said Bud. "By the way, you responsible for getting me out?"

The detective nodded. "Two more people were killed here, flipper tracks and all."

"So, I heard." Bud shook his head as he peered out into the Gulf horizon. "You know, despite all that's happened here, I had to stop by one last time before leaving."

"You going miss this place?" asked Jensen

"Yeah, I will, but not the nightmares," said Bud. "Those unfortunately will follow me no matter where I end up."

"And where will that be?"

"I'm headed to North Carolina. Got a brother who lives in – get this, Transylvania County. Ain't that a kick in the nads?"

Jensen laughed. "Another good word." The two clinked bottles.

The man smiled. "I know a few."

Stiletto Hell: Sole Survivors

It was late April. Harold Bailey, stiletto attack survivor, woke up with that queasy feeling in his innards. For months, he'd contemplated spilling the truth to his family about that fateful Halloween Eve, but knowing how inconceivable his encounter was with the satanic shoes, he could not divulge a word.

"No," he said, gazing at his reflection in the bathroom mirror after a brisk tooth flossing. "I can't risk losing my job or causing my family any embarrassment."

On one occasion, after downing a few beers at a block party, he half-jokingly spilled the beans to his next-door hipster neighbor. The man thought Harold's fictitiously wild tale would make a truly awesome movie.

In the end, he simply tucked the 'incident' deep beneath the pine floorboards of their vintage colonial. The sanitized version where he simply stumbled over his daughter's plastic unicorn toy in the middle of the night would have to suffice.

***

A couple of weekends later, on a partly sunny Saturday afternoon, Harold's wife Kathy managed to pry him away from watching Yankee baseball. Harold owed his wife a full afternoon in the Big Apple for destroying her skyscraper devil-red stiletto heels (not to mention a pair of kitchen tiles).

The two drove to Hoboken then took the PATH Train to Greenwich Village in New York City. The two had lunch at Ray's Coal-Fired Pizza, splitting a medium cheese pie littered with black olives, onions, and green peppers. They sat outside, café-style, sipping on their matching Dos Equis amber lagers.

Afterwards, the two browsed a cavernous used bookstore sandwiched between two competing antique shops. Harold ended up purchasing a vintage copy of *National Geographic*, a 1968 February issue titled *Sharks: Wolves of the Sea*, along with a fine, leather-bound edition of Charles Dickens, *A Christmas Carol*, one of his favorite tales.

After stepping outside, Kathy's cellphone rang, chirping loudly like a mockingbird. "Hello? Oh hi, Christina. Hey, you'll never guess where Harold and I are. What? No, we are not at Chucky Cheese."

Christina Watkins, art teacher and good friend of Kathy's, had finally returned to work after spending months recovering from a savage badger attack. Visible scars still ran along her arms and legs.

"That's great you're in the Village," said Christina, longing to return to the city herself.

"What are you up to this weekend?" asked Kathy.

"I'm just hanging out, lounging on the sofa with Brody," answered Christina, snacking on sea salt pita chips. "Doctor says I should be able to start kick boxing again."

"I still can't believe how badgers got into your house and ambushed you like that; it's like something out of a bad horror movie," said Kathy.

"I know, tell me about it," replied Christina. The two chatted on and on as the Baileys strolled along the city sidewalks.

Harold glanced up at the sky and noticed grayish clouds rolling in. He cursed himself for not bringing along an umbrella. They stopped at a corner intersection then proceeded to amble towards a small park with a playground. Kathy gave her friend a play-by-play as they strode past a slew of street venders.

"Whoa, check out the daggers on these babies," commented Kathy, catching her reflection in a pair of gleaming crow black stilettos off a line of folding tables covered in rich colored tapestries.

"Oh my gosh, Christina, you should see the shoes they're selling near the sidewalk. You would love them!" said Kathy, now wondering if this was the place Christina had purchased the red stilt walkers. She turned towards the owner. "I'm sorry, ma'am, what's the name of your store?"

The middle-aged woman with distinctively pale skin and long black locks was finishing up a transaction with a young woman. Her abundance of silver bracelets slinked up and down as she gestured with both arms. "Thank you and have a most eventful day," she said. Her excessive eye makeup made her look an Egyptian goddess, albeit one on the raccoon side.

"I'm sorry darling. How may I help you?" replied the woman, turning to Kathy.

Kathy spotted the sign hidden behind a pair of towering knee-high hot pink camouflage patterned boots. "Oh, here it is. Never mind," she said, in a cheerful voice. Kathy was savoring her venture into the Village, away from her exceptionally dull suburban life. "Madam Celeste's Sidewalk Shoe Emporium. Ooh, I like that. Christina? Hello?"

Christina sprang up from the sofa, her cat leaping off her lap with an annoyed drawn out meow. A wave of trepidation shot through her mending limbs. "Uh, yeah, that's the place," she replied nervously. "Hey, can I speak with Harold for a second, real quick?" Kathy handed the

163

phone over to her husband as Madam Celeste began sharpening her sales pitch.

Harold stepped away out of earshot and leaned up against a lamppost. "Hi Christina? How are you feeling?"

Despite the aches, Christina began feverishly pacing the floor in her living room. "Harold, you *cannot* let Kathy buy anything from that store, you hear me?" Harold wasn't keen on his wife buying any type of shoes with a heel over an inch high, not in the least.

"Listen, Harold," barked Christina, getting his attention. "That's where I bought those shoes, the red stilettos for Kathy and a pair of sharkskin stilettos that tried to eat me like freaking Jaws. I don't know how, but those shoes are pure, unadulterated evil!"

"Hold on," said Harold. "You were attacked by stilettos too? Sheesh. "Just when you thought it was safe to go shopping."

"Hell yeah," shouted Christina. "what happened to you?"

Harold stepped away from the crowd for more privacy. "I was getting my laptop from the bedroom when I heard a clicking sound coming from the closet. I opened the doors and those red stilettos started attacking me. I ran to the bathroom where they almost finished me off!. I ended up torching those bastards in the fireplace! And you?"

"I was getting dressed, ready to go out when I cut my finger. A harmless paper cut! But it set off the sharkskins something fierce. I'm lucky to be alive."

"Where are the shoes now?" asked Harold, "Did you kill them?"

"No, but I managed to stuff them in an old backpack. I filled it with a few bricks and tossed it into the pond behind my house," said Christina. "I still have nightmares about those feeding frenzied shits."

"Yeah, you and me both," said Harold, eying his wife browsing at one of the tables.

Christina added. "I ended up destroying all thirty-five pairs of my prized high-heel shoes. You know how hard that was for me? Now I'm wearing flats for God's—!"

"Holy moly," Harold interrupted. "Kathy's reaching for her purse! What do I do?"

Christina paced back and forth. "I know, I know. Tell Kathy you'll buy her a brand new pair of those poopy-brown duck boots she likes so much. What's that catalog she drools over?"

"Uh, L.L.Bean?" he answered; glancing down at his own pair of duck boots he was wearing.

"Yeah, L.L.Bean! Tell her you'll buy her *two* pairs and something flannel. Just get her away from that crazy lady!"

"Okay, okay," answered Harold, not a person of confrontations. He stood there, staring at the creepy woman, his mouth partially agape.

"Hurry!" cried Christina.

The whole scene unfolded in slow-motion: Suddenly, there was Harold, his healed thigh wound beginning to throb. He stumbled towards the line of folding tables filled with shoes, a battalion of sky-scraping styles and colors that now seemed to be staring at him – like they knew that *he* knew that . . .

"No, not those!" hollered Harold, as he spotted his wife fondling a racy pair of tangerine orange stilettos with bold black tiger stripes adorned across the front.

The owner, dressed in her ruby-red paisley dress, grinned a toothy grin. "And dearie, I've got a BOGO today, two for forty dollars." She glanced over at Harold with a fluttering wink, her fake eyelashes big as awnings.

"Wow," said Kathy, now reaching into her purse. "I could buy two pairs for my friend, Christina!"

"I'm sorry, did you say, Christina?" said Madam Celeste, raising her right brow.

"Yep," Kathy replied. "She enjoys shopping for stilettos here in the Village."

"Noooo," bellowed Harold. He felt like he was moving through quicksand as he launched himself towards his wife, intercepting the transaction. He grabbed Kathy's hand and pulled her away from the cash register. The two stormed down the block and out of view of Madam Celeste.

"Harold Bailey, what the hell was that all about?" said Kathy. "I wanted to buy shoes for Christina."

"Trust me, honey, Christina wants absolutely nothing to do with those shoes. In fact, it's safe to say she'll never ever set foot – no pun intended, in any shoe from Madam Celeste's Sidewalk Shoe Emporium."

"What are you saying?" said Kathy, dumbfounded. "They're just shoes."

"No, they are not," blurted Harold. "That Celeste lady planted some sort of evil curse on those shoes!"

"You're worrying me, Harold. A curse? Really?"

Harold took his wife over to a green metal park bench facing the single lot park. A handful of children were frolicking on the swings. "Do you want to know what really happened to me and your friend Christina? I mean the whole truth?"

"Uh, you told me you fell on a unicorn toy and Christina said she was ambushed by badgers."

Harold felt like pulling out his remainder of his hair. "My God, honey, does that even sound remotely plausible to you? I mean . . . badgers?"

Kathy paused. "Come to think of it, they are quite rare for our neck of the woods." Suddenly, the light bulb started brightening. "Oh my."

Harold explained in fine detail the strange truth of what really transpired that Halloween Eve. He even relayed Christina's account.

"You mean she was attack by her sharkskin stilettos," said Kathy. "She loved those shoes."

"Not anymore," replied Harold.

With Kathy's stunned, jaw-dropping look solidly in place, Harold stood up and bought a couple of sodas from a hot dog vender and sat back down. "Here you go."

"Thanks," said Kathy. "Maybe you should buy something stronger."

Harold glanced at the children playing and turned back to his wife. "Look, I know this all sounds cuckoo bananas, but it's all true, I swear. I still have the wounds to prove it. And now your friend, Christina."

"So, there was no devious unicorn toys or killer badgers?"

"No," replied Harold,

Kathy took a sip of soda and sat up straight. "You know Christina did mention something strange about her shoes."

"What was that?" asked Harold.

"She thought she saw them . . ."

"Move?" guessed Harold.

"Yeah," answered Kathy. "I thought she was just kidding around; you know her."

Harold took a drink of soda. "The scary thing is there may be hundreds of people out there who have been attacked, or maybe even killed by those damn shoes. And that Celeste lady is behind it!"

"It's so preposterous," replied Kathy, a sensible, even-heeled type through and through. "So you're saying that anyone who buys those shoes . . ."

"Now we're on the same page," said Harold. "Anyone who buys those psycho stilettos is in harm's way. We've got to stop this insanity, now."

"What do you have in mind?" said Kathy. "Walk up to Madam Celeste's Sidewalk Shoe Emporium with a flame thrower and toast her inventory to a crisp?"

Harold took another drink of soda. "That would do it, but too many people would notice."

"That they would," smirked Kathy. "Should we find a police officer?"

"I don't think New York's finest are going to believe us," shrugged Harold.

"I know what we can do," said Kathy.

"What? What?" replied Harold, anxiously.

"Follow her after she packs up her things."

"And then?" said Harold.

"I'm not sure," replied Kathy, "But we can at least find out where she lives."

"Are we talking a stake out?" surmised Harold.

"I guess so," said Kathy, suddenly feeling like she was in a *Scooby Doo* meets *Twilight Zone* episode.

"Excellent!" said Harold, finishing up his soda. "We'll wait here and then tail her in a cab. From there, let the shoes fall where they may."

***

It was nearing seven in the evening. The Baileys stood just outside a corner deli under a canvas overhang trying to not look suspicious. They nibbled on their second bag of M&Ms with peanuts to pass the time. The two peeked around the chipped brick wall and spotted the mysterious Celeste as she pulled up in a late 1990s eggplant purple Dodge Caravan spewing cloud gray exhaust.

The peculiar woman scuttled back and forth until her car was filled to the brim with her devilish inventory. She pulled away from the curb, smoke billowing out from the dangling tailpipe. The couple quickly waved down a cab. Thirty-five minutes later, Harold and Kathy found themselves in a rundown neighborhood in Union City, New Jersey that fostered a distinctively dreary vibe.

The bleak evening sky helped to hide the two amateur sleuths as they slinked up next to a telephone pole three houses down. They watched as Madam Celeste backed up the minivan into the driveway leading to a neglected two-story corner lot property. In the back was a dilapidated whitewashed barn.

The two moved up to the corner of her property, hunkering down by a ratty hedge and leafless maple trees.

Madam Celeste parked the minivan a few yards from the barn door. She got out and looked suspiciously around before unlocking the shiny metal padlock with a key. Harold and Kathy patiently waited as the woman proceeded to unload the shoes, making multiple trips before creeping inside herself.

The two waited what seemed like hours hidden in darkness. A light drizzle began to fall. "Damn, I knew I should have brought my umbrella," said Harold. "What are you doing?"

"Just checking up on the kids," answered Kathy. I said they could watch a scary movie and make macaroni and cheese."

"Fine," whispered Harold. "Hold on, which movie?"

"*Evil Dead II*. Our trustworthy son says it's funny."

Let the nightmares begin, thought Harold. "Okay, let's move." The two sneaked up to the side window of the barn, out of view from the house. Harold stood up and peeked through the corner of the dingy glass.

"What's she doing?" asked Kathy.

Harold squinted. "I can't see much, the window's kind of grimy."

"Hold on," said Kathy, who pulled out an extra napkin she had stuffed in her jacket pocket from the pizza restaurant. "Here, try this."

Harold wiped away a silver-dollar-sized spot. "Much better, Thanks."

He peered deep inside. There, in the center of the squared room were shoes – dozens and dozens of shoes.

And against the wall were loads of boxes, all stacked nice and neat.

"My God, she's got a warehouse in there," uttered Harold.

Madam Celeste came out of a back room and finished setting up her evil inventory, displaying them in circular seating style.

"Well?" persisted Kathy, tugging on her husband's jacket. "What's happening?"

"The shoes are lined up like fans at a sporting event," said Harold, giving a play-by-play.

"Pardon my French, but that sounds a bit fecked up," said Kathy.

"You're telling me," said Harold. "Hold on, she's doing something."

In the center of the coliseum of shoes sat a plate-sized terracotta bowl brimming with a low-lit fire. Madam Celeste started chanting in Latin, repeating the same verse over and over again. She sprinkled the flames with a dark powder. The flames erupted. She shouted higher, her chanting reaching intolerable decibel levels. After ten minutes, Madam Celeste collapsed to her knees in exhaustion and bowed her head. The room was in total silence.

"It looks like she's performing some kind of twisted ritual. Now she's on the floor, praying I think," observed Harold.

"Praying?" asked Kathy. "Praying to what?"

Harold couldn't take his eyes off the woman. "This is too weird." A minute passed.

Suddenly there was a lone tap on the weathered barn floor. Then another.

"Hold on, I hear a noise," said Harold. Kathy stood up, the suspense killing her, and sneaked a peek while standing on a cinderblock.

A few more taps followed. Madam Celeste remained in the same position. There were a few more taps then…BOOM!

The room erupted like thunderous snare drums. The chorus of circular shoes hammered away on the wood planks like piano keys. Louder and louder they stomped, settling into a rhythmic pattern.

Madam Celeste seemed to feed off the deafening noise. She started to sway, gazing up to the rafters, her arms outstretched. The woman revealed a wicked smile, baring her crooked teeth.

The rows of shoes clomped up and down, maintaining their place. It was flat out mayhem. The shoes kept pounding away. The whole rundown structure rattled. Madam Celeste laughed hysterically. The sound was utterly intense.

Kathy and Harold bent down, cupping their ears. Harold raised his voice. "We need to come back here later tonight with reinforcements." Madam Celeste shifted her eyes towards the window and snarled.

The two scattered, jogging a few blocks before hailing an Uber back to their parked car in Hoboken. On their way back, the couple devised a plan involving matches and lots of gasoline.

***

After discussing the matter over dinner, the couple hired a neighborhood babysitter to stay with the kids. Harold borrowed Kathy's phone and called Christina, explaining their plan in fine detail. She had no issues seeking revenge on Madam Celeste and expunging her wicked stiletto collection off the face of the Earth.

After midnight, Harold and Kathy swung by Miss Christina's home six miles away in their reliable silver Toyota Camry. The night was miserable with scattered rain followed by patches of blanketing fog. Kathy frowned, but Harold and Christina didn't care. Despite stepping into uncharted waters, the two shoe attack victims were itching for payback. They felt invigorated, almost like superheroes ready to defeat an archenemy.

On the way to Madam Celeste's home, Harold and Kathy reviewed their game plan again with Christina, gasoline and all.

"So, we're gonna try and set the night on fire," mused Christina.

"Funny, Christina. Let's just hope everything works out by the end of the night," countered Kathy with a wink.

Being overly cautious, Harold parked the car a block away from Madam's house. They got out, braving the elements in their matching black attire. Harold popped open the trunk and retrieved the dulled red metal gas can.

Christina came equipped with a pack of small wooden matches of her own. "Where does the witch live?"

"It's that dreary looking house at the end of the block," pointed Kathy. They passed six homes before reaching their destination. A perpetual shade of gloom adorned the corner property, isolated from the other houses.

"Christ, where did this lady get her home decorating tips from, *The Munsters*?" joked Christina. Kathy snickered while Harold offered up a feeble laugh.

The three huddled behind shrubs and a rusted chain link fence that separated the neighboring vacant lot. The long trail of twisting metal led to the back yard, butting up against a five-foot high cinderblock wall. They sneaked along the damp surroundings before reaching a pair of soaring deep green pine trees, everything else on the property in perpetual gloom.

The three then scurried over to the side of the barn, crouching beneath the familiar side window Harold and Kathy peered through earlier.

"This is where that whacko cooks up her batch of killer Kates and pernicious Pradas," whispered Christina.

"I'm assuming those are shoe brands?" smirked Kathy.

"Maybe villainous Valentinos, heinous Hush Puppies, or baneful Badgleys?"

"Enough, Christina," said Harold. "This is serious."

"Sorry, sorry," answered Christina. "Hey, I want payback too. You realize that lady cost me my pinky toe – and it was so cute too, along with my favorite toe ring. It was a gift from my mother, you know."

"It was really cute, Harold," Kathy added.

Harold stood up slowly and peered into the window before backtracking. "Hold on, your mother gave you a toe ring for your birthday? Isn't that kinda weird?"

"Not if you like toe rings," she grinned.

Harold shrugged. "You got me there."

His thigh wound throbbed again as he pointed the flashlight inside the barn. The shoes were still, hundreds of them, still lined up in circular rows. The fire was out, but a slight haze of smoke still hovered in the murky interior.

Kathy stood on her tippy toes and peaked in. "Looks like she's not there."

Harold took a glance around the front of the barn and noticed a padlock on the door. "Rats."

"What's the problem?" asked Christina.

"There's a padlock on the front door and the back door appears to be boarded up."

"So?" said Christina.

"What do you mean, so?" snapped Harold. "Do I look like a guy who can pick a lock? That's not exactly my forte."

"He can't even figure out my bra strap," kidded Kathy.

"Well, I've had some experience with locks – and don't ask for any details," quipped Christina, who took out a slender black case filled with assorted pointed instruments. "My other specialties include mixed media and papier-mâché."

Christina moved ahead and crunched down at the door, ready to pick the lock when a pair of floodlights came on. "Damn motion sensors." She scampered back around the corner and hunched down with Harold and Kathy.

"Shoot, I should have noticed that," said Harold. "Sleuths we are not."

"Of, course we aren't," exclaimed Christina. "You're an accountant for God's sake, and I teach kindergartners how to trace their little hands to make Thanksgiving turkeys."

"Well, we've got to resolve this once and for all," said Harold. "Those shoes are killing innocent people, and apparently, that sicko Madam Celeste has no problem with that."

Harold rummaged around the yard and picked up a sizable fallen branch. He slinked back over and peeked up at the beaming lights. As soon as they shut off, he jumped out and gave them a thwack. "Alright, instant darkness," he quietly boasted.

"I'm impressed Harold," said Kathy. "That was a heck of a leap."

"Thanks honey," replied Harold.

Christina scampered over to the front door again. She took out her line of tools and began tinkering with the padlock like a dentist removing gunk between a child's braces. Kathy played lookout at the side of the barn. "Any progress?"

"Almost there," replied Christina, her tongue askew in focused determination. "Got it!"

She unlatched the lock and signaled to Harold and Kathy. "Let's move."

Harold closed the door holding the gas can as Kathy turned on the flashlight. All three stood there, stunned by the audience of shoes. "Let's do it," said Harold.

Harold began racing around the ring of footwear, starting in the center. He drenched each and every pair with gasoline as his wife directed the beam of light.

"I can't believe we're actually doing this," uttered Kathy as Harold finished up dousing the high-heeled killers. She spotted the orange tiger print models, so harmless earlier in the day, now potential killers.

"Are we good?" asked Christina.

"I think so," said Harold. "Let's see if there's anything else in here."

The two checked out a back room: nothing but broken up old wood furniture and a makeshift workbench. As they headed back to the main room, Kathy noticed a light emanating from the house.

"We've got to leave, now!" said Kathy. "Oh no."

"You see her?" asked Harold.

Kathy turned milk white. "No, but we may have a bigger problem."

"What's that?" asked Christina.

"Those tiger stilettos," pointed Kathy. "They're not on the shelf anymore."

"Kathy, hide in the back room," ordered Harold, "Christina and I will handle this."

"You hear that?" paused Christina. "It sounds like . . . purring."

Suddenly, the door burst open. There, standing alone and draped in black, was Madam Celeste, standing over six feet tall in her fuzzy stiletto slippers.

The tiger stilettos simultaneously jumped into her cradling arms. She began caressing them in James Bond villain fashion.

"Normally, my customers don't survive shoe attacks, but somehow both of you managed to do so."

"Sorry to disappoint you," snapped Christina.

"And this is a first," smirked Madam Celeste, shaking her head. "A man who wears . . . oh hell, I don't judge – I only kill."

"Hey, I don't wear stilettos," snapped Harold, "I'm strictly a Puma guy!"

"Did you say . . . Pumas?" grinned the woman. "Oh, I think I have a pair of those just for you, along with my other big game cat collection. I see you've met my Bengal beauties."

"May I ask why you are doing this?" asked Christina. "I mean, cursing all these beautiful shoes. What did they ever do to you?"

"Oh, I have my reasons," Madam Celeste replied, cunningly. "Let's just say it's payback."

The pair of Bengal tigers leaped to the ground, inching towards Harold and Christina in a stalking motion. The deep orange shoes twisted and turned like they were ready to pounce. In the blink of an eye, the tiger stilettos were joined up by a pair of leopards and cheetahs.

"Don't do this," pleaded Harold.

"Such enlightening words from such a vertically-challenged person. No, you and your wife hiding in the back room and Miss Christina here must die – and be sent straight to heel."

"You mean hell, send us to hell," corrected Christina.

"That was humor, Miss Christina" said Madam Celeste, who suddenly began sniffing the air like a hound dog. "What were you three planning to do?" Her lips curled, eyes narrowing. She closed her eyes, balled up her fists, and screamed. "Attack!"

Harold and Christine bolted for the back room and joined Kathy, who slammed the door shut. Harold propped up a broken chair just below the doorknob as dozens of heels pierced the rotted wood, nearly busting through.

"Awake, awake, my footwear of hellfire. You shall reign supreme as we conquer the world and then seek to…"

"Go to hell, psycho bitch," yelled Christina.

"Watch out!" yelped Kathy as more heels stabbed though the door.

Harold scrambled for any weapon he could find. He picked up an old mallet from the workbench and pounded away at the sealed back entrance. "We gotta bust out!"

"Maybe ram it with your shoulder," said Christina. She picked up a loose plank of wood and tried to cover the many holes. Another direct hit and the shoes would be inside for sure.

"Together," suggested Kathy to her husband. Together they charged the door. Smack! They backed away and crashed into the door again. "One more time, Honey!"

"Hold on," uttered Harold, inspecting the door. "We broke it! He raised his leg and kicked out pieces of old wood.

"It's clear! Let's get the hell out!"

As Christina turned, she was struck just below the shoulder by the tiger stiletto. She screamed in pain as blood streamed from the puncture wound. "Help!"

Harold and Kathy rushed back and pulled the sharp-edged heel out.

"You little shits!" grimaced Christina holding her shoulder as Harold grasped the mallet and pulverized the orange stiletto. Kathy helped Christina up and the three dashed through the back door.

"Wait," uttered Christina. She handed Harold the box of matches. "Take 'em; you know what to do."

Harold helped her to the front corner of the barn. "Hold on, I'll be right back. He busted open the front door catching Madam Celeste by surprise.

"Hey, Celeste," shouted Harold, "Your sole is mine!" He lit a handful of matches and tossed them in the direction of the gas-soaked shoes. A circle of flames sparked up immediately. As he bolted outside, Harold closed the door and placed the padlock back on the hinge, locking it.

Madam Celeste, standing near the ceramic pit, howled like a caged animal. Harold peered through the window as all the shoes stomped in unison.

Harold backed away to join Kathy and Christina when he paused, realizing he was potentially killing a human being. That would be hard to live with. He ran back and gazed inside the side window. "Oh my God."

Madam Celeste began flailing like a whirling dervish. The shoes suddenly began attacking her from every direction like thrown darts. In moments, she was impaled all over like a pincushion. She dropped to her knees desperately trying to shield herself from the onslaught.

The crazed woman lifted her head and spotted Harold through the window. "I curse you all to death!"

Harold glanced through the window, staring as the lone tiger stiletto approached Madam.

"No please! I gave you life!" she cried as the Bengal stiletto crept closer, mere feet away.

In a split second, the stiletto shot from the floor and finished the murderous woman off, square between her eyes.

"You live by the shoe, you die by the shoe," uttered Harold, grimacing at the lethal act.

Suddenly, all the stilettos made an about-face towards him. "Uh no." He ducked as the high-heeled shoes slammed against the barn wall. "Time to leave!"

Harold ran to join Kathy and Christina at the end of the driveway, and the three headed back to the car. Harold pulled away from the curb, but instead of driving away, he made a U-turn and headed back to Madam Celeste's property.

"What the hell are you doing?" said Kathy, "We got to get out of here!"

"We will, we will," Harold replied, as he parked the car across the street. "I just want to make sure no shoes escape."

They sat across the street as the barn toppled over in flames, all pumpkin orange and fire engine red. Harold watched intently as the sound of wailing sirens approached. He turned to Kathy and Christina.

"Promise me no more fucking stilettos."

"No more fucking stilettos," replied Kathy and Christina in unison.

Harold smiled, putting the car in drive, and drove away.